Deadlight

Lasher Lane

PATTERAN

Patteran Press
Studio City, Calif. 91604

ISBN 978-0-615-76705-5
LCCN 2013906728

Cover illustration by Jane Kil
Cover Concept Design by Jane Kil

Manufactured in the United States of America
First printing April 2013

ACKNOWLEDGMENTS
To Rob Bignell for his invaluable expertise and guidance; my
friend, S.R. Mallery for her unwavering support; my family,
especially Jane and Arun for their wisdom of technology; and Ann
Williams for her mutual love of "Pleasant Valley."

DEDICATION
To my father, Curtis von Dohln who left before he had the chance
to say goodbye.

AUTHOR'S NOTE
Regarding historical references, I am obliged to acknowledge
both Douglas E. Hall's *Images of America: Edgewater* and
Lynn Fox's *A History of the Borough of Edgewater.*

Foreword

"A score or so of men are spoken of around town as rivermen. This word has a special shade of meaning in Edgewater: a riverman not only works on the river or kills a lot of time on it or near it, he is also emotionally attached to it—he can't stay away from it."

—Joseph Mitchell, "The Rivermen"

I have long been inspired by Joseph Mitchell's short story, "The Rivermen" and later by authors such as Lynn Fox, Douglas E. Hall, and Cheryl Solimini, who portrayed my small town of Edgewater in a positive light. But I was just as much inspired by Ronald Sullivan, The New York Times reporter who chose to define our off-the-map, harbor town in a negative light, accusing us of possessing a "blue collar mentality," "spirit of isolation," and "mistrust of outsiders."

I remember the words "solar deprivation," a phrase he'd coined in his 1975 article: "Edgewater, New Jersey Finds High-Rises Casting an Unwelcome Shadow" being tossed around town, and I wondered, along with my fellow residents if the effects on our behavior from the loss of sunlight were real.

From across the Hudson, Mr. Sullivan had taken the time and trouble to concern himself with our riverfront refuge, hemmed in by the 200-foot towering Palisades and the menacing monstrosity of high-rise buildings that sat atop them like giant dominoes ready to tumble down at any moment, crushing us into oblivion. A lot of us laughed at the notion of his choice of words, defining our symptoms from living in shadow, saying we suffered from "collective psychic depression," "physical sense of oppression" and that "the psychological wound was daily." Even though I was one of those laughing, I couldn't help being haunted all these years by Mr. Sullivan's article.

Once regarded as "New Jersey's Barbary Coast," the libation-loving town had at least eighteen taverns occupying its mere four-mile-long, two-block-wide borders. But along with those taverns, the grittiness of industry, and the loss of sunlight, there also was the counterbalance of rustic beauty, the majestic waterfront, and the rural privacy the town afforded. Being born and raised near water, we were often referred to as "river rats" and proud of it despite the effects "solar deprivation," real or imagined, might have had on us.

These days, if you look between the overcrowded waterfront development, which in some places sadly resembles facades from a scenery backlot, you'll find traces of the charming Edgewater that once existed, which include the Dutch Cemetery from the 1600s, where an Indian princess is laid to rest, along with the man who ferried George Washington back and forth across the Hudson during the Revolutionary War. My family's marina, owned for decades by my cousins Joseph and Pat, is still there, and is the place where my grandfather and his brother made and raced canoes and designed paddles for the early Twentieth Century Olympians.

I'm not sure if the ghost of George Washington was ever sighted in my town, but I've heard countless stories about the Lenape seen roaming Old River Road late at night.

Prologue

With a pint of vodka as my new daily crutch, I sat studying the corner of the boathouse, trying to forget that night. Ripped out, the barge's gaping hole created the perfect rustic picture frame for my own personal view of the seagulls, the skyline, and the little forgotten red lighthouse obscured by the great bridge that joined two states, two very different world—five minutes apart.

Through the boathouse opening, I watched seagulls as they sat on pilings, all of them facing the direction of the bridge as they confronted the wind with their wings tucked tightly behind them. I envied their freedom and ability, having both wisdom and courage to come and go as they pleased without ever having to answer to anyone. I watched them glide effortlessly past the sylvan shoreline, following the Hudson on their way back to the Atlantic, oblivious to those of us below who were forced to rely on maps and tide charts.

Always cool and dark, this boathouse was my favorite place at the marina, and the spot I'd visit whenever I wanted to be alone. But as hard as I'd try, the luxury of being alone no longer seemed possible since my life had been forever changed as a result of that one fleeting moment, his one careless, inconsiderate act. For some reason, he had singled me out and wouldn't let me forget. He was there to remind me almost every day of that tragic and horrific event.

This is Where I Belong

I f you listened carefully enough, you could hear the roar of Manhattan from this New Jersey town like a constant breath being exhaled across the Hudson. Although Pleasant Valley was a common name for many U.S. towns, this Pleasant Valley was different. At times it seemed dark to insiders, but often dysfunctional and in the dark to outsiders.

The town sat at the river's edge, was only three miles long and nestled under the mighty bluestone cliffs of the Palisades. Supposedly, hundreds of millions of years ago when violent forces of nature broke up the great super-continent, what was to become New Jersey was at its center, probably the only time in history New Jersey would ever be the center of anything other than a bad joke. Out of this violence, the Palisades were born accidentally, but they served as a beautiful backdrop for the out-of-sync and off-the-map little riverine town with its farms and fruit orchards, shady lanes and single traffic light.

I never understood why the *Metropolitan Times* had bothered to write an article about the place, one so insignificant and small that it had been purposely left off of maps. The article said that the town's inhabitants, which I guess included myself, felt inferior and depressed because it was decided by a few professionals looking down on us from the cliffs above that we all suffered from "solar deprivation," the cause being that each day the town was being deprived of a few extra hours of sunlight because the massive cliffs that served as a backdrop for it had blocked the light out.

According to the *Times*, this lack of sunlight accounted for the rampant alcoholism, depression, drug abuse, and lack of ambition that had always plagued Pleasant Valley. Whatever the reason, the blue-collar town with its taverns on every corner was certainly a haven for dipsomaniacs because no matter which direction you entered, north or south, you'd have no problem finding numerous establishments that sold alcohol. The *Times* would have the surrounding area convinced that between the lack of sun and abundance of taverns, the town's inhabitants were like the many sunken ships lost under the river being puller deeper and deeper into an abysmal sludge, never to return. Was it the fault of the hard-working German and Irish-Catholic immigrants? According to outsiders, by them migrating here, it had only seemed to grace the tiny town with second and third generations of genetic drinkers born into a fog that would linger for decades. And as the decades passed, it was obvious to those outsiders that we all had become the good-for-nothing blue-collar sons of our good-for-nothing blue-collar fathers. We, however, were fine with our taverns and ourselves.

And even though ironically we were the smallest part of one of the richest counties on the East Coast, Bergen County, we were the aberration, the puzzle piece that never quite fit.

***

"Don't ever take this river for granted," my grandfather would say. "Someday when you grow up, if you move away, you'll come to miss it." I knew he was right. I had always loved the Hudson, even with its brackish wakes of PCBs and hospital amputations. It wasn't always this way. My grandfather had known this river in a different time, before the bridge was here, and he said that in winter, the Hudson was so clean that it froze eighteen inches thick and people would skate or race their ice yachts fearlessly across it to get to what was on the other side: New York City.

As I stood looking through the hole of the boathouse, a massive, wooden, floating leviathan of service that was really a cavernous covered house barge, I imagined the days of the ice harvesters.

Many were farmers forced to settle on the seasonal work as a means to feed their families. After cutting the 10' x 20' "ice cakes" from the frozen river, they would push them with poles through narrow man-made canals to the waiting icehouses, which could store 50,000 tons at a time with only sawdust to keep the ice from melting. I thought of the tremendous hazards of standing on the ice with a horse drawn ice planer as a powerfully intense river coursed beneath their feet, many dressed only in their street clothes as protection from the harsh winter conditions, as both men and animal risked death by drowning with the horse's only protection a rope around its neck and the men, nothing. Sometimes the men worked all night to keep the canal from refreezing. The "cold gold" was so clean, all that would have to be removed from it—using formaldehyde—was the urine left by the workhorse. These days, the abundance of toxic filth from industry wouldn't allow the river to fully freeze and had even infected the shad, a longtime livelihood of the local fishermen.

My grandfather spent a lot of his time on the Hudson. As a young man in the early 1900s, he left his only family in Yorkville to purchase this small stretch of land he'd noticed across the river.

Because of his love for boats, he built a marina here, hired a permanent crew, and with their help began making canoes, paddles, ice sails, and ice yachts that could travel "a mile a minute." It took a lot of skill and patience to fashion canoes, grub boxes, spars, leeboards and paddles out of wood.

He'd often use cedar, ash, mahogany or maple. Hardwood paddles, he said, were preferred by the more experienced canoeists with better upper body strength. Hardwood also allowed for thinner blades and small handles that wouldn't break under pressure. So that he and his workers wouldn't break under pressure, every day at 4 p.m. without fail all work was interrupted for what he liked to refer to as "communion." "Down with liquor!" he'd say raising his shot glass, and the whiskey bottle would be passed around. It didn't matter what god the men worshiped or who they prayed to at night; it was a religious experience that none of them could refuse.

***

What was it that my grandfather had seen that made him want to stay when he first came upon this little river town that sat so inconspicuously at the bottom of those cliffs? An introduction to insignificance. A mapless haven. Yes, I know that "mapless" isn't a word you'll find in any dictionary, but if there were such a word, it would perfectly describe that location and us, its inhabitants. But maybe that's what my grandfather had always been looking for: some sort of campestral seclusion.

It was a town whose historical happenings were known only to the locals, and rarely, if ever, mentioned in history books, and one that would include the 1910 discovery of a fossilized phytosaur.

But simply because New York City had the museum to house the remains would mean that they would take all the credit for its find by saying it was discovered there, across the river. They'd even be so bold as to go ahead and name it Rutiodon Manhattannensis adding further to our off the map irrelevance.

Everyone from our town also knew of the French Huguenot who was credited with starting a settlement and ferry service that would aid George Washington and his troops when they fought several battles against British troops during the Revolutionary War. There is even evidence of those battles being fought off our shores in a painting by Dominique Serres, painter to King George III, illustrating the soldiers as they stood on the town's ferry dock. But you would never know by looking at it now that this lush and sleepy little town was once witness to a violent history much worse than the Revolution. More than a hundred years before Washington's army would arrive here to fight for their freedom, and more than 300 years before my grandfather would come to choose this very same location to reside, there would be total devastation and death unleashed upon a particular sea captain's parcel of land. Before Pleasant Valley, the area along the riverbank that runs under the Palisades was a patroon settled in 1640 by Captain David de Vries, which he called "Vriessendael."

The Lenape, or "original people," who had settled here thousands of years ago on the banks of the "Muhheakantuck," or river that flows both ways, would come to welcome him as a trusted friend who also would rely on them for trade. Long before Henry Hudson or George Washington or even the

Dutch captain himself would venture to this abundantly green and majestic place, this land was their bucolic paradise. They felt secure living under the Palisades, and it's been said that they always believed the cliffs that formed a wall behind their home were raised solely for protecting them. They not only used those cliffs for shelter, but they also sought refuge keeping close by them, especially during the long, harsh winter months, in huts made from bent saplings, grasses and bark. Holes were dug in the ground at the center of these huts to serve as fire pits to provide for cooking and warmth with another hole in the roof that served as a chimney.

They hunted beaver, raccoon, deer and bear but never crow. They regarded the crow as sacred and for this reason it was never to be used as food. Legend has it that way back in ancient times before there was winter, the crow's feathers were every color of the rainbow. Then the time arrived when the Snow Spirit came to Earth and all the animals and people became so cold that they didn't know how they would ever get warm again. The crow was sent up to the Creator to ask him to make the snow and cold go away. The Creator couldn't unthink his thoughts about winter, so He took a stick and poked it into the sun until the wood caught fire. Then he gave it to the crow to bring fire back to Earth to make everyone warm again. As brave Rainbow Crow flew downwards, he carried the stick of fire in his mouth. Because of this, all of his feathers were burned, and that is why the Indians believe they are still all black today.

The fur-bearing animals that the Lenape hunted were needed for clothing and trade. To make clothing, they would use sharp rocks to skin the hides, and to repel the rain they would attach turkey feathers with a tight bark netting to the hides. They fished shad, giant oysters and sturgeon that were larger than a full-grown man so big that they could have easily been mistaken for those enormous sea monsters so often illustrated on ancient maritime maps. But their way of life, including the valley that they and their friend, Captain de Vries, knew and loved, would forever be changed. It wouldn't be long before their pastoral refuge would quickly become a sanguinary inferno in which the sky would be lit with fire and the river would run red with blood.

They would soon learn that they had much to fear from a man named William Kieft, who had arrived from Holland to become the new governor of New Netherlands, or what the Lenape thought all along to be their own island, Mannahatta. He was nothing like Captain de Vries or most of the Dutch they had traded with in the past. With no regard to whether it was legal or not, Kieft came to consider land on both sides of the Hudson under his jurisdiction. He wanted no friendship with the "savages." He only really cared about obtaining furs for profit, not the welfare of the Lenape. He would trick the Indians into thinking that if they paid him on a regular basis, he would have his Dutch soldiers provide protection for them from other tribes in the area. Along with furs and corn, he demanded they pay him frequently in their money: black or white clamshells, the black being worth more. The Dutch had lived in peace for years with the Indians. They had gained a mutual trust and respect for each other but because of Kieft's greed, the Lenape continued to fight him over land ownership and trade and soon grew to hate him. It didn't take the new governor long to find reasons to go to war with them, especially after an elderly immigrant who was his friend was found murdered. A farm animal that was seen running free was also considered to be stolen by the Indians.

Many settlers, including Captain de Vries and the men who worked for him, didn't want to go to battle with the Lenape. This forced Governor Kieft to appoint a council of twelve men from the surrounding communities to vote on whether or not they should go to war. Unhappy that war was voted against, Kieft disbanded the council and brazenly ignored their decision. He came up with a secret plan and found a group of loyal soldiers to carry out his wishes. While he stayed on the opposite side of the Hudson, his men would cross the river at night to the side that would later become known as New Jersey, where they would attack the Lenape as they slept. Fire was set to their homes. Children were ripped from parents' arms and hacked to pieces while they watched helplessly, then the children were thrown into the fire or the swift current of the river. Parents who jumped in and tried to save them were not allowed to come back on land and drowned. Some children were bound on planks and mutilated. Those Indians who escaped decapitation, drowning or fire fled to the woods and hid there during the night until it was quiet and seemed safe to come out.

By early morning some returned with limbs missing, while others held their entrails in their hands, as they tried in vain to seek help from Kieft who had made an appearance in Vriessendael the morning after to survey his men's work. The ones that survived had thought they'd been attacked by another tribe. They stood in shock and disbelief, confused when Kieft admitted that he had ordered his own men to carry out such atrocities. What Kieft had failed to realize was that long before he and Captain de Vries had come to this place, the Lenape had already been trading furs with the Dutch in exchange for not only bullets and guns but alcohol, which along with the firearms they'd acquired through trade, would add to their confidence when it came to retaliation of more than a hundred Indian lives lost. All tribes from the lower Hudson Valley would band together in a furious three year attack on the Dutch that would greatly reduce the number of settlers. And Captain de Vries would lose everything. He returned to his homeland heartbroken, exhausted, and against his will. The West India Company who had sent Kieft to be governor of this new land had recalled him, but his ship would become lost at sea. Ironically, he would meet the same unfortunate fate he had imposed on some of the Indians: death by drowning.

***

Three-hundred years later, there is no evidence of the Indians or the giant sturgeon; only the piles of oyster shells they had discarded, crushed by centuries of pounding tides, and the shad that had now been poisoned by industry. According to local legend, the only other thing supposedly left of their tortured souls are the tribes of revenants often seen walking aimlessly on Old River Road late at night.

The Lenape had felt security in being somewhat hidden away

from the outside world by the 200-foot cliffs behind them, but I wondered if they, too, ever felt smothered by them. Were they also considered victims like us? Victims of stolen light? According to the press, we were. But if we were all suffering, I don't know if any of us realized it...or cared. When industry came to the south side of town, an urban grittiness accompanied it, and along with that an air of apathy and nonchalance.

The town never had been concerned with image or whether or not it had one. It didn't care if it wasn't included on any maps. It didn't sit in awe of the city it faced. It wasn't the typical picture of small towns everywhere, which are so often painted as sleepy and naïve. Sleepy and naïve it never was, with its murders and mob violence during the coal dock strike, deaths from chemical factory explosions, and drug trafficking, not to mention, over 40,000 cases of whiskey smuggled during prohibition into this country from the Bahamas by way of Pleasant Valley. During Hitler's reign, there would often be secret meetings held by members of the German-American Bund who would travel across the river from their home base in Yorkville to clandestine locations on the waterfront, which not only made my grandfather feel on edge, since he coincidentally just happened to come from Yorkville and now was the owner of a waterfront location, but a lot of the town as well, especially when the FBI had come knocking on doors, looking for the exact locality of these Nazi meetings on the river.

Still, through all of this each of us remained hidden away from the rest of the world and had come to echo the same sentiments of apathy and nonchalance, generation after generation, but I wasn't sure if we were ready to accept the one the press had chosen to bestow upon us...depression.

Slip Inside the House

M y dad never seemed to mind being born into the business of boats. He loved them as much as his dad, but with each hurricane season that passed, he wasn't sure he'd have enough energy to get through the next. One year, we lost whole barges and docks that were swept away as if they were just leaves in the wind. Mom and dad had the patience of saints when it came to starting over and literally picking up the pieces, but they needed more than patience since the insurance company rarely ever matched what was lost.

The marina hadn't really grown much since the days when my grandfather was well enough to run it. Although there were definitely a lot of inboards, cabin cruisers and even some yachts, mostly all of the canoes were gone. But compared to the other surrounding marinas, it hadn't changed with the times; unlike the others, it didn't have a lot of amenities. We also lacked enough water pressure and electricity to serve every boat in every slip, and the area was in desperate need of dredging because at low tide all the boats sat on mud. When the tide went out, the river suddenly became like a giant bathtub of dirty water that someone had pulled the plug to let drain, leaving behind not only mud, but the incredible stench of wet silt.

Owning the marina hadn't made my dad a wealthy man, but he loved his job anyway, and loyal customers tended to put up with what they saw as minor inconveniences in exchange for his friendship. Over the years, it not only had been a gathering place for a lot of old salts, but I'd heard an escape from their nagging wives as well.

***

Old River Road separated the marina from our house, which was also old, from the 1800s, and sat on a dead-end street. I'd often hear upscale neighborhoods refer to dead-ends as cul-de-sacs, but Pleasant Valley was a blue-collar town, so there were no fancy names about a street that had one way in and the same way out. It was simply known as a dead-end.

The house was built by a young sea-captain who supposedly met his untimely death in an attempt to rescue his cat that had climbed a tree during a thunderstorm. He was in no way related to the Dutch Captain de Vries from the 1600s. At one time, the town was full of sea captains who were all still in town, but in the local cemetery. If you ever decided to visit and took the time to read their gravestones, you'd notice most had actually died from drowning not electrocution. It was hard to tell which of these ghosts my brother swore he would see on a regular basis. I would have to guess it probably was the one who had built our house and was hanging around not realizing he was dead, if you were the kind who believed that sort of thing. Ike, a family friend, claimed to know about spirits and their antics, and always said that spirits, because they're made of electricity, often were seen more frequently in places by large bodies of water...and everyone knows that electricity can move easily through water. As far as spirits, though, I had always been a skeptic, but certain events that occurred would soon have me changing my mind.

The house was a bi-level gingerbread of white clapboard and dark green trim. It was drafty and old; not really scary looking for a Victorian, but more scary sounding with its hissing radiators, creaking floors, and rattling windows. The front hall had a large staircase with a massive black mahogany banister the young, unfortunate captain was supposed to have gotten from the inside of an old whaling ship. There were no switchplates on the walls to turn the lights on, only pull chains in the center of each room. It was frustrating, not only trying to find your way in the dark, but also in cold weather when touching the metal chains caused painful shocks from static electricity.

In the basement was a root cellar with a dirt floor where field mice could easily come and go in the winter. Besides the clanging furnace and hissing radiators, you could hear them scratching and scampering between the walls as they'd try to escape from the cold.

In the backyard, there was a well that was surrounded in summer by Lily of the Valley and Bluebells; its cover was a heavy square made of slate. The fresh water well fed from a stream in the Palisades and ran underground until it mingled with the salt water of the Hudson. On the right side of the well was a pear tree by the fence that separated our yard from our neighbors, the Kellys. Under that tree was where my grandfather kept an old teak canoe from his racing days. He kept it for sentimental reasons more than anything else, since he was too old to use it. When we were a lot younger, Will and I would turn it over and sit in it, pretending to be on some adventure until my dad would see us from the window, and yell at us to leave it alone.

There were apple and peach trees, and a twenty-foot pine tree that had lost a lot of its branches on the inside. The outside branches were still intact all the way to the ground, which made it feel like a large, round shady room if you stood underneath. Will and I decided when we were little it was a great hiding place, a place to go and think when we wanted to be alone and escape from the rest of the world.

***

Besides my grandfather's, Pleasant Valley was home to quite a few marinas. Some had been forced to relocate from Manhattan when the West Side Highway was created. In the early twentieth century, they each had their own canoe clubs and would race one another for trophies. My grandfather's marina had quite a few canoes at the time and also took part in the races.

Before the George Washington Bridge was here, in the days that preceded the automobile, people would take their canoes all the way upriver to a place called Buttermilk Falls, and since the water was so clean then, most of the riverfront towns actually provided bathing beaches so you could pull your canoe right up on the shoreline to picnic or swim.

Around that time, there was also a film studio in town, and silent movies were often filmed in the area because of the scenic cliffs and river. It became a sanctuary in summer for such celebrities as Enrico Caruso, D.W. Griffith, and Theda Bara. Sarah Bernhardt even owned a hotel in Pleasant Valley. For a brief and fleeting moment— during the time of the silent motion picture—it seemed that the town was the Hollywood of the East. But all that would change because of the town's proximity to the river. Industry saw an opportunity and slowly crept in. Soon, factories that made coffee, aluminum and automobiles would make their homes here, not to mention a sugar factory that would draw rats as big as cats. On the south end of town, blue skies and green trees would be replaced by cement structures that coughed out black smoke and benzene. The town would even acquire its own menacing heartbeat supplied by a colossal behemoth: the largest aluminum mill in the country. Its thunderous pounding pulse resounded day and night, never missing a beat, thirty years and counting, as it rolled out sheets of metal that could stretch for forty-five miles. Coal-fired steam trains from Pennsylvania and Appalachia would bring coal from mines to fuel the industry of Pleasant Valley, leaving behind not only coal, but covering the entire town in soot. With the storage of hydrogen and dynamite, industrial fires would be commonplace. Toxic and hazardous chemicals that were not only needed to make aluminum but also PCBs, coal tar, and ammonium nitrate, would seep into the groundwater, posing a threat to every Pleasant Valley resident for generations to come.

***

Almost seventy years had passed since the marina was built. Ike, my grandfather's sidekick, was not only the most experienced boatman at the marina, but also the best shad fisherman in town.

His clothes were always tattered and salt-stained, and he'd wear an old moth-eaten wool hat every day, whether it was winter or summer. He had those eyes that wrinkled up at the corners and smiled at the same time his mouth did. He'd tell you more times than you'd care to remember that he was raised on "graveyard stew," which he confessed, to my horror, was a combination of stale bread soaked in milk. Sometimes the milk was sour, but being as hungry as they all were, they ate it anyway and didn't complain. He said it was usually used as a remedy for the sickly. He wasn't sickly, he'd stress, while drawing on his meerschaum pipe; he just happened to come from a large family with "too many mouths to feed and too little money to feed them."

Ike loved the smell of gasoline from the boats in the morning; he equated its aroma to a cup of good, strong coffee. He'd start his day by bending over the gas dock, and with his hands, he'd wash his face in the river water. The gasoline made oily rainbows in the water, and that was the spot he always went for.

"How can you do that?" I'd always ask him with disgust.

"It's what keeps me looking young," was always his answer.

He'd been a friend of the family forever, it seemed. Since my brother and I were little, we'd sit and listen while he told us scary stories about the Spuyten Duyvil or "Spouting Devil," where the Hudson and Harlem rivers meet; a place where the undertow was so strong that it would take men's lives. He'd tell us stories about the ghosts of the Lenape Indians whose poor slaughtered specters were forced to walk Old River Road for all eternity, or about Blackbeard, the pirate whose ghost was always trying to remember where his treasure was buried, or the ghost of the man who hid in the grandfather clock from British soldiers during the Revolutionary War. The reason Will liked hearing those stories over and over again was because Ike would insist that not only were all of them true, but that they all took place right in town. If I had to bet on any of them being true, I'd have to bet on the Lenape story. But I had grown too old for ghost tales, even if my younger brother hadn't.

I was named Henry Hudson Cline, and even though I was in no way related to my namesake, my parents had such an affinity for the river we lived by that they thought there was no better moniker to grace me with. It was quite a handle, and unfortunately I was stuck with it. But there were much more important things to think about than hating my name...like the draft.

It was 1968, and the U.S. government couldn't decide who it

was more afraid of: hippies or Martin Luther King. Two things I'd noticed they were clearly not afraid of were going to war and using napalm, both of which had regrettably become household words. But then, there were those who gave us hope: the growing number of youth who opposed the idea of war and made us realize that it was alright to question authority and OK to be individuals not sheep. And whether the Beatles realized it or not, they had instilled a newfound freedom-from-fear mentality with their music, including songs like "All You Need Is Love." But the U.S. military would continue to ignore us as it sang its own song, "Napalm Sticks to Kids," while they proceeded to drop almost 400,000 tons of the stuff on the Vietnamese.

My brother Will was 16, two years younger than me. He didn't have to worry about ever getting drafted. Born with a brain injury, my brother would always be the eternal child, yet for most of his life children shunned him. He eventually learned to stay out of the way since he'd soon find society easier to observe from the outside looking in, like some alien studying earthlings. I often thought that the road ahead of him would prove to be much harder than being drafted into any war. I'm glad he had a best friend besides me, though, and that was our dog, Fritz. He was a mutt, a brown and white terrier mix with extremely short legs. He refused to walk on a leash, and when we tried to put one on, he'd just lie down with his front paws covering his ears and wouldn't get up until we gave in and took it off. We also could never leave him alone in the house or yard because he had a fondness for wood, and if left alone too long, he'd been known to eat the rungs out of ladders and make rocking chair legs straight. When neighbors fussed about termites in their houses and the damage they'd done, mom just rolled her eyes. I got the feeling that mom secretly hoped he'd run away some day on his own. And even though she was tempted, she'd never be the one to leave the gate open, since she knew Will and Fritz were inseparable.

There were two other things that my brother also couldn't seem to be without: one was a small plastic statue of St. Christopher that he always carried with him in his pocket, and the other was his friend, "the Captain," someone he swore would visit him regularly, but someone we could never see no matter how hard we tried.

Fresh Air

I was always amazed to see things return to life after being crushed under the weight of the snow all winter, only to emerge an exact replica of themselves when spring came. It meant that the Earth had come alive once again. There seemed to be a definite and deliberate cruelness to winter on the East Coast, so cruel that it seemed almost hostile, and at the same time inhospitable to not only man, but nature itself. In all its painful, frozen bleakness, winter was like a cancer and spring its cure.

When the shad came upriver, no one cared that they were riddled with PCBs. Their arrival wasn't only a riparian right of spring but also a rite. The older, more seasoned fishermen could actually predict their runs by whatever happened to be blooming on shore at the time. The bright yellow flowers of forsythia were first, and they signaled the beginning of the season when the ocean fish entered the river, as they did every year to spawn like salmon. Next came the magnolia, dogwood and serviceberry, or shadbush which signaled the peak of the season. And finally, the lilac which denoted not only the end of the season, but also the biggest and best catch.

The shad were often caught by moonlight with lines that laid deep in the Hudson and were the original ones that were fished for over 150 years. Passenger ferryboats had to make sure they'd go out of their way not to get snagged on the lines and nets.

Both the fish and the roe were North American delicacies that had served as an East Coast food source since even before the Revolutionary War, as far back to a time when the Indians depended on it. Cooked the settler's way, which was by "planking," the fish were nailed flat to oak planks with bacon and then placed above glowing coals that melded the distinct flavors of oak and shad. The fragile caviar of this fish—known as the roe—was prepared separately and ever so carefully.

Spring was a busy time at the marina. People readying their boats were very anxious to get them back in the water after a long, languorous winter, while others came and went on the docks pumping gasoline and carrying ice chests to beat the tides in and out. On weekends when we didn't have school, Will and I earned money being put to work sanding and painting boats, scraping barnacles off their bottoms, or repairing loose boards on the docks. When things were slow at the marina and Ike could spare us, we'd take a small aluminum rowboat upriver to visit our friends, Steven and Jane. Without question, St. Christopher had to come. Ike had given Will the little plastic statue years ago, and of course since Ike loved telling stories, he told Will the story of St. Christopher, whose real name was Offero. Ike said that he had things in common with Will. They both lived by a river and liked to help people. The saint would offer to carry those that couldn't make it by themselves across the river on his back. The story went that one night Offero carried a small child across the river who kept growing larger and heavier with every step. When they reached the other side, the growing child told Offero that he was really Jesus, and that Offero had just carried the weight of the world. Jesus then told Offero that from that day on, he should change his name to Christopher, which meant "Christ-bearer."

***

Even though we were both baptized Catholic, we rarely went to church anymore, so I don't think faith was the reason Will chose to keep the plastic amulet with him; I think it had more to do with him liking Ike's story. I don't know if it was the child that magically grew part of the story that fascinated him, or if he really thought that St. Christopher had the power to protect him from danger.

Whatever the reason, Will had come to rely on him as his good luck charm. Funny that in all my younger years I'd been forced to take religion lessons after school and attend church, but not once did I hear Offero's story. From my experience, the priests spent most of their time admonishing or threatening the congregation and making us recite phrases that included "The Holy Ghost," which would always incite giggles from my childhood, non-Catholic friends—and I have to confess—even some of my own faith. Not only that, but all the kneeling and doing strange hand movements in unison with our fists and index fingers could be quite a workout for some of the elderly churchgoers.

If the saint wasn't in a locker in the boathouse, he was in Will's pocket. And on the boat, the tiny plastic man went in a secret compartment only Will and I knew about, a storage space that we had built into the base of a seat. It was mostly used to protect our things if we happened to get caught in the middle of a rainstorm.

Despite our determination, Will and I could never get very far by rowing. It was always too tiring to paddle against the formidable current. And the oars, since they were made of wood, definitely distracted Fritz and he'd always try to catch them, barking and growling as they came up out of the water. If we stopped to rest for even a few minutes, the current took us back again almost to the point where we started. If we really wanted to get anywhere against the current—or with Fritz—we'd always have to relent and use the outboard.

The heat of the spring sun would reflect off the metal boat, as we felt the bridge like a giant magnet pull us under its shady expanse. We cut the engine and decided to take a break. As we sat in the middle of the river underneath the bridge's vast rumbling shadow, the roar from the traffic above us was deafening. I looked up at its dizzying height—at least 200 feet above us—and thought of those people that, for one reason or another, sadly decided to take their lives and actually had the courage to jump. I thought of how I'd heard that some newspaper long ago had held a contest to name the bridge when it first opened, and "Gate to Paradise" was one of the names suggested. I wondered if those who jumped knew that, and if it might have held some kind of mysterious allure for them like members of some arcane ceremonial suicide club. I also wondered if right before they jumped they'd given any thought to the poor family members who'd be forced to identify them after the river eels and fish had made their way through every bodily orifice.

I asked Will how high he thought the drop was from where we were to the bridge's deck above.

He didn't know. I explained that hitting the water from that height would be like hitting concrete. I asked him if he thought someone would survive a jump like that. He just stared up at it with his mouth open. Before Will had a chance to reply, Fritz barked his answer—either that or he wanted to know why we or the oars weren't moving. With the help of the engine and a close eye on the oars, we started moving upriver again toward Steven's and Jane's house.

Steven and Jane lived with their parents in a charming and rustic section of town known as the Colony. The area was first inhabited by Dutch settlers in the mid-1600s. A century later, its inhabitants would find themselves unwilling hosts to Hessian soldiers that would not only demand food and shelter but also would use the settlement to cunningly hide from Washington and his army as he was being welcomed, at the same time, by other settlers like the family who owned the ferry service, all the while Washington's troops unknowingly within very close range of the houses where the Hessians were deliberately evading them.

In the early 1900s, the area would again be recycled for the main purpose of providing housing for hardworking German and Irish immigrants who came to America on a quest for that cliché, fairytale promise of what most of them believed was supposed to be on the other side: greener grass and a road more golden.

The side of the town where the Colony was located, in fact, had always been the greener side. It had always been spared factories. But no matter what side of town you were on, industry had made the river that bordered the town unfit for swimming. The irony was that in the days when the area sheltered the Dutch and the Lenape together, Hessian soldiers, and finally, poor immigrant families, the river was extremely clean and the land cheap. As decades passed, the houses and land that sat right at the river's edge were considered waterfront property and far from cheap. No one cared that the river had become a graveyard for toxic chemicals and body parts donated by hospitals and organized crime.

Since the river was constantly moving at a rapid pace in opposite directions, you couldn't see how dirty the water really was. The dirty water didn't make the Colony any less charming, with its riverside cabins, towering balsam trees, and twisting dirt lanes. Early mornings, when the mist came in off the river and mingled with the balsam, it created a fragrant fog much more intoxicating than anything you could ever roll between two Zig-Zags and smoke.

Beyond the dense grove of trees and quaint cabins, the land stretched out to the waterfront and a narrow stretch of coarse sand beach. Patches of goldenrod and Queen Anne's lace shot up here and there between small rocks that glinted with mica, along with the scattered remnants of oyster shells left by the town's earliest settlers. The larger rocks were boulders that had separated themselves from the Palisades long ago and tumbled down to the river's edge.

Today the air was hot and quiet—almost too quiet except for a pair of buzzing dragonflies that passed like miniature aircraft above our heads. But even with all the quiet, it was obvious there was a storm coming. I could see the darkening sky behind us, as we tied the boat to our friend's dock. Trees on the Palisades were turning their leaves inside out as the wind was starting to pick up. I had been out on the Hudson once in the past during a sudden thunderstorm, and I had the unfortunate experience of being chased by lightning bolts I had seen gaining on me in the distance. The river was no place to be, especially in an aluminum boat. Out in the middle, it could get as rough as the ocean with tall waves, fierce wind, thunder and lightning. Fritz began to bark loudly at the restless trees, and even though it was annoying, I couldn't complain since he spared us the oars for the way back.

Steven called down to us from his bedroom window that he and Jane would be right out.

Fraternal twins, they looked nothing alike. Jane had long, ash-brown hair and blue eyes, and there was something about her mannerisms and features that reminded me of a young Grace Kelly. For as long as I could remember, I had a thing for her, but that was my secret. Steven was blond with brown eyes and still hadn't outgrown his adolescent awkwardness. Although he was quite shy, Jane was very outspoken and never minded telling people what they wanted to hear. She told it like it was, even though she found from experience that usually no one wanted to hear it.

The three of us would be turning eighteen, but being born a girl, she wouldn't have to worry like we did about being drafted into a war she didn't believe in. Even so, she had assured Steven and me that if we were, she had a plan. If her car could make the drive, she would take us to Canada, and going by the media coverage of the violent bloodbath in Vietnam, who could argue with her?

She drove an old, gray Mercedes sedan with a vacuum shift that she bought from some car mechanic who offered no warranty. She didn't care, for her the car was love at first sight. There was no clutch pedal—supposedly way ahead of its time when the car was new—but there was a 5-speed shift on the steering column. The car had a start button, a temperamental choke, an 8-track player and a sun-roof. It also had a mind of its own. It would start when it wanted and take off when it wanted—regardless of when she used the gas pedal—which could be pretty scary when attempting to merge onto a highway, and sometimes, without warning, there weren't even brakes. But with all that it put her through, she was very proud of it, even if it did give her more trouble than it was worth.

While I saved for my own set of wheels, Jane was my ride to school, and she'd gladly pick up any other senior stragglers along the way who were "too cool" to ride the school bus, that is, when we actually chose to go to school. We'd usually all start out with good intentions, only to end up driving around listening to music or being the first in line at the nearest mall to buy concert tickets, or sitting in some diner for hours, where, when we should have been discussing the talents of Chaucer, Poe, Miller and Bierce, we were happier discussing the musical talents of Waters, Barrett, Baker and Bruce, or which Lee was more gifted: Arthur or Alvin; all of us experts in the new and exciting music that seemed to come out of nowhere, but sadly at that point in our lives experts at not much else.

We'd missed so many days of school that when "senior cut day" was near, to our surprise, we would be informed by our teachers that should we decide to cut that particular day we might risk not graduating. That meant we, along with half the school it seemed, would have to start applying ourselves and getting much more serious about things other than music...and getting high.

***

The town's many taverns—eighteen in a 4-mile radius, believe it or not—provided places that we, the so-called "depressed and solar-deprived" residents, could frequent, especially when they provided an escape from the oppressive heat and humidity of East Coast summer days. When we were bored, we'd go visit Lenny. Besides being the only bartender at the Lookout, he also owned the place. It had a great view of the Manhattan skyline that offered a cure for our boredom. And even though none of us were eighteen yet, Lenny felt if we were old enough to fight in Vietnam then we were old enough to drink but not the hard stuff, only beer and wine.

As the thunder in the distance got closer, we'd make it just in time to beat the sudden spring downpour. The inside of the Lookout was dimly lit, and had what most old taverns seem to have in common: the enticing smell of stale spilled liquor. The walls were knotted pine, and the floors were covered in sawdust. One long window ran behind the length of the bar that looked out onto the river, the bridge and the city. In the early 1900s, the tavern not only served alcohol but was also a burlesque house that provided much needed entertainment for weary, exhausted workers when their shifts ended at the many factories along the riverfront. These days, it was mostly an old man's bar, that is until Lenny introduced "Happy Hour," and then business started to pick up. For recreation, the tavern had a pool table and pinball machine, plus a jukebox that let us play as many songs as we wanted for free, since it was rigged to play with the same quarter that magically reappeared in the coin return every time three songs were selected.

Lenny never seemed to mind that Fritz came inside with us, as long as he stayed away from the pool sticks or anything else that was made of wood. I think that's the reason why Lenny always gave Fritz a small saucer of beer when he visited. Hoping to protect his assets, the second he saw us coming through the door with the dog he'd get the saucer ready, not only to calm Fritz down but to make him forget there was any wood in the place.

On that particular day, we were the only ones Lenny was serving except for three guys who were seated at the opposite end of the bar. I recognized them as Eammon Dunn, Mike Hale, and John Kelly, my next door neighbor. John looked our way and acknowledged us by holding up his glass, and as I expected— tough guys that they were—the others didn't. Even though John's friends always   seemed to be either getting into trouble or looking for a fight, he still chose to hang out with them, which was beyond me.

John was the kind of guy you could hate and feel sorry for at the same time. I couldn't really blame him for the way he was, considering the kind of life he had at home. He wasn't just an only child but unfortunately the only victim of his father's frequent fits of rage due to alcohol abuse.

Mr. Kelly was a retired New York City police officer who had moved his family across the river to New Jersey hoping for a quieter kind of life. That was his version of the story, but around town the story went that the police were finished with him. He had been caught propositioning prostitutes, then exploiting and harassing them, and threatening them with jail time if they didn't supply information about the pimps and drug dealers on his beat. He saw to it that if they didn't comply, the women would be arrested for soliciting a policeman, when it was really the other way around. He wanted to look like the best cop with the most information, when instead he turned out to be the worst, but not by much. The force asked him to resign quietly, and gave him an ample cushion to get rid of him, fearing that more corruption from the department might surface if other rogue police officers happened to be exposed.

He'd soon find out that "retirement" left him with way too much time on his hands. And ever since he'd moved his family across the river, strangely enough, alcohol—as it had been for generations of others in Pleasant Valley—had suddenly become his new hobby. His policeman days were long gone. Those days he felt like he had a reason to wake up every morning, instilling in others what he knew in his heart was nothing more than a false respect born out of fear in those he only referred to as "the filthy scum" that roamed the streets of the city he regarded as his own.

When it came to John, he constantly reminded his son that he had to marry because John was an accident, that he could never measure up in his eyes. And he would never be cop material; he cried too easily. As if when John was a young boy, burning his leg under the kitchen table just for a reaction with the hot spoon Mr. Kelly used to stir his coffee was some kind of prerequisite for becoming a policeman, some kind of toughness test. Over the years, the test seemed to work, only not the way Mr. Kelly had intended. John had learned to fight back with the only weapons he knew he had: apathy and silence. And they proved to be pretty powerful weapons because John noticed the more apathetic he became to his father's torture, the less he was abused. It got to a point where Mr. Kelly realized that he could no longer derive pleasure in doling out physical abuse, but that didn't stop the mental abuse from coming. There were many nights when the sound would carry from next door, as Will and I laid awake listening to him screaming at John.

Mrs. Kelly was apathetic, too, since communication with the man was lost years ago. After many years of marriage, she finally learned it was best to remain silent around him except for only the most necessary one-word replies. In the beginning, when John was a lot younger, she'd come to her son's defense, but now she was just tired—tired of Mr. Kelly, their marriage, her life.

He had died suddenly a year ago, which meant John and his mom could relax a little, except for when it came to income since most of the money Mr. Kelly had been left from the department had been squandered on off-track betting and drink. The burden was now on John to support the family.

But he wasn't even out of school yet, and the part time jobs he'd gotten in the past he had never been able to hold because even though he hated his father and didn't want any of his attributes, he had managed to inherit one, and that was his love of alcohol.

I remember being at Mr. Kelly's funeral, watching John and Mrs. Kelly as they went through the motions of a grieving family, but their grief didn't seem genuine. It almost seemed like they couldn't wait to get the service over with and get him in the ground.

***

John and I went to different schools. Because I had a Protestant father and a Catholic mother, my parents sent me to public school but compromised by forcing me to endure what quickly became for me hell on earth...or catechism. With each passing day as the years went by, I would grow more convinced that the Catholic Church was the institution solely responsible for my possible social anxiety disorder that would probably follow me throughout life. I don't think there's a self-help book out there yet that could ever repair the damage my ego had suffered at the hands of demonic, chastising, rum-soaked priests and crazed, uptight masculine nuns. I couldn't imagine John, with he being a Catholic school student full-time, having to endure this treatment both at home and school with no escape. At least I had a sense of calm until the bell rang to signal the end of my public school day, before the start of my religious lessons, to begin to feel the dread. The nervousness that the church imposed upon so many of us at such a young age always seemed unnatural and unnecessary to me. Not only that, but the younger Catholic school kids didn't help our confidence by running into their houses every day when they saw us public school kids coming home for fear, they'd claim, of actually catching some weird disease if we happened to so much as even glance in their direction.

The older ones—the seniors like John and his friends—were the ones we'd have to prove ourselves to physically, because after them being reprimanded by priests and nuns all week, they'd only feel compelled to demonstrate all the lessons they had learned about "brotherly love" on us. And they had learned well. By that, I mean they were quite adept at bashing your skull in or knocking your teeth out. Only if you happened to be male and went to public school, or had just moved to town, were you required to go through an initiation: an arranged fight between yourself and someone who was expressly chosen for you, mainly because of this person's ability to beat you senseless. If however, you beat your opponent senseless, you were welcomed wholeheartedly into the group. If you lost, you were scorned for life. Also, they were so used to taking on out-of-towners who just happened to wander into town, either by accident or deliberately, that there was never a question in their minds who would win; they'd had years of practice. But one time they were taken by surprise when a new guy from an all-boys school in New York City—not some small suburban town—came to town all prepared.

When he showed up for his own initiation, he wore a tin can in his pants as a shield to protect his private parts, since he knew they'd be a definite target, proving he had more experience than any of them ever could have imagined. He won the fight, and from then on was never tormented and always respected as one of the gang.

To this day, I had somehow gotten away with having to go through the process myself. Maybe the reason I always seemed to be spared the initiations was because I was John's next door neighbor, and at one time, his close friend. He never seemed to bother me. In fact, John never seemed to bother anyone. He would act tough by suggesting who should be provoked, or he'd instigate a fight, but whenever there was an actual fight, he'd always just be in the background watching.

***

Back at the Lookout, I tried to avoid listening in on John's conversation with his friends, but it was becoming increasingly difficult since the more they had to drink, the louder they became. I couldn't believe it when I heard John betting Eammon and Mike a thousand dollars that he could jump off the George Washington Bridge and live to collect the money. So they wouldn't suspect my eavesdropping, I kept my eyes straight ahead on the window, with its view of the skyline and the bridge. And as I looked at the bridge in question with its 200-foot drop, I thought to myself that a thousand dollars, even a hundred thousand, didn't sound like much for a stunt like that.

In the past, the bridge was occasionally used for the purpose of intentionally ending one's life but never a bet. I couldn't think of anyone that was foolish enough to ever jump and think they'd actually live to collect some reward. Maybe what John had in common with those victims was that he was also drawn to it but in a different way. Maybe he felt he was untouchable, invincible enough to taunt and elude even death, yet able to win a bet at the same time. Then again, maybe in his heart he secretly knew that he'd have no chance, and that's why he had decided to do it. It was an easy way out in the end, looking more like a brave stunt that had resulted in an accident rather than suicide.

I suppose living close to any landmark long enough, whether it's natural or man-made, becomes for some of us a motive force in our lives. In a way, we find comfort in the same habitual scenery being there in front of us every day. The familiar mountain range, ocean or river, bridge or tall building not only becomes part of our everyday lives but part of our identity. But sadly, none of us have any control over the fact that this inanimate object or landmark—unlike us—has the capacity to remain on Earth centuries after we're gone.

So I couldn't understand his newfound obsession with the bridge. I hoped that his reckless Houdini bravado would wear off when the liquor did. But with John, when did the liquor ever wear off?

And even as I sat there thinking that, I could see him out of the corner of my eye pushing his empty glass forward on the bar to get Lenny's attention.

Jane had already played the same Merilee Rush song three times in a row on the jukebox. Steven was playing pinball, and Will was asking Lenny for more cherries to put in his Shirley Temple. Lenny was obliging my brother, but at the same time he was ignoring John and his empty glass, yet listening, like I was, without being too obvious, to the conversation John was having with his friends.

"All we need is a boat," John said, deliberately looking in my direction. "I jump, while you guys wait in the boat underneath the bridge. If I win, I get to keep the money. If I don't—but I will—then you guys get it."

"Hell, count me in!" Eammon said. "This is easy money."

"Nice bunch of fucking friends I have!" John said, as he smiled to himself and waited for a refill.

He impatiently tapped his empty glass on the bar, loud enough for Lenny to hear.

Stunned by what she had overheard, Jane let the jukebox stop playing. I knew, like all of us, that Lenny also had heard their whole ridiculous plan. He turned and accidentally dropped the jar of cherries. Except for the sound of glass hitting the floor and the thunder in the distance, there was an awkward silence as he glared at John and his friends.

He then yelled in their direction, "That's it! You three are cut off! Go home and get some sleep, and come back when you can all make some sense!

There's an easier way to earn money than jumping off bridges, you know!"

Jane looked over at me, her eyes wide. Will only cared about the cherries on the floor and was down on his hands and knees trying to retrieve what had spilled. Still seated on his barstool, John was angry that he'd been cut off, so he attempted to push himself away from the bar with his hands. The stool, balancing on its back legs, crashed to the floor. He hit his head hard and was knocked out cold for a few seconds. Lenny came around from the back of the bar to help him, but as John came to and his friends lifted him up, he put his hands out in front of him to refuse Lenny's help. Then he pulled away from his friends and brushed himself off, stumbling out the door as Eammon and Mike followed closely behind.

Lenny looked at me and said, "Those guys are trouble. Don't you go getting yourself involved in this by giving them a boat. I've got a good mind to call Mrs. Kelly right now and tell her about this jackass plan of his to try and kill himself. And another thing—" Lenny tried to look serious as he pointed to Fritz who was lying on his back, sleeping by an empty saucer and some chewed-up wood that was unrecognizable—You owe me a pool stick. Don't you ever feed that dog?" I had to admit that if there was wood anywhere, drunk or not, Fritz would find it.

Mr. Soul

For a lot of the country it had been a violent spring. Bob Dylan's song, "The Times They are a Changing" certainly seemed to have come true. With April came nationwide riots in response to Martin Luther King's assassination. Trenton—one city like many—mourned his death with a seething anger. Rioters shattered glass, hurled rocks and set fires. Some even helped themselves to golf balls from sporting goods stores and drove them up Trenton's Perry Street into the heads of policemen who quickly found it necessary to borrow little league helmets and welding masks as protection. Things got so desperate at one point that blacks against whites became bricks against bullets.

When things finally calmed down, I didn't know if it was just my imagination, but the government seemed relieved that Dr. King and his quest for peace and harmony were no longer a threat. All that was left for them to worry about was their other fear... hippies. If hippies were actually something to be feared, then I guess you could say that Carl was definitely one of them, although he'd argue that fact; he'd much rather be called a "freak."

Carl was twenty-two, four years older than I, and the only child of well-off parents who were both thrilled when their son was accepted to Cornell. A few months shy of graduation, he decided to drop out. He not only dropped out of school, but out of sight...from them and everyone else. He made a decision the day he walked out of school to go on a permanent sabbatical from the corporate "rat maze" and never have anything to do with manmade institutions again—especially schools, churches, the military; the law, and sadly the world of wealth his parents represented. His favorite expression was "so what," and as far as he saw, it should pertain to every aspect of life.

Having a positive effect on all age groups of the female gender, most women and girls saw him as helpless, sensitive, handsome and charming. He had shoulder-length brown hair, a little longer than the Beatles or most other bands wore it then, that kind of hair that really seemed to turn the opposite sex on. And they always wanted to know what was on his mind since he constantly had this dreamy, faraway look in his eyes. But I think the look was probably due more to the fact that he was perpetually high rather than really deep in thought.

Everyone called his house "the Castle" because of the high stone walls that surrounded it but mostly because evenly spaced on those walls sat massive gargoyles, each with their own frightening grimace. It wasn't a castle at all but an old fortress that was actually used once by Hessians spying for the British during the Revolution. This castle sat in a densely wooded area on top of the Palisades overlooking the river. The stone walls were thick with wisteria. Once you got behind them, there was a path that led to narrow circular winding steps made of the same stone and a very old cemetery with just a few small markers; the writing on the graves was illegible, almost completely worn off. At the top, there was a large grassy yard with a gambrel-roof Dutch Colonial, also made of stone, in its center.

Enshrouded by enormous shade trees that helped to keep the area well hidden, the yard was encircled by yet even more stone fashioned into arches notched out of the hillside, which centuries ago had the sole, crucial purpose of serving as lookouts for spies keeping tabs on Washington's troops.

Carl had the house inside sparsely furnished with a few threadbare oriental rugs, two paisley chairs and a sofa, also threadbare, that could once be described as velvet. There were bookshelves, a fireplace, some artwork that was given to him by his friends from Greenwich Village, and a stereo system that seemed to be the main focus of just about everything since it was considered the most important item in the house.

He didn't rent or own the place; the town just ignored the fact that both he and the house were there. There was no electricity or running water to wash his dishes, clothes, or himself for that matter. For this, he used the stream that ran by his house; the same stream that also fed not only my backyard well but most wells in town, although his use of the stream in winter was pretty limited.

He existed on a barter system between friends who were mostly starving artists or musicians and would linger like a bunch of friendly squatters after his infamous parties, sometimes for months at a time. Week to week, he'd barely scrape together enough money for food, liquor and weed, although to him, liquor and weed would always take precedence over food. The gas and slip for his skiff were free and supplied by my grandfather in exchange for chores he did around the marina. That's how we met. Carl was the first person I'd ever seen walk a boat into a marina. One day he had been drifting out on the river, not sure of his exact location. He'd ignored the tide charts, and when he wanted to find out where he was, or what town he was in exactly, he thought he'd attempt to enter our marina, not realizing the area was badly in need of dredging, which made dealing with low tide even worse. He found it so low that his boat became stuck in the mud. He couldn't row or even turn the engine on, and since he'd run out of gas and the money to pay for it, he rolled his pants up, and with a rope in his hand, he bravely jumped overboard, wrestling and struggling with his boat, while at the same time battling the putrid, black primeval mud that was trying to suck him under. He won out and made it to the gas dock, talked my grandfather into some free gas, and since he'd arrived just in time for "communion" found himself with a shot glass in his hand and the promise of a job. My grandfather's health might have prevented him from doing any real work around the marina, but he'd never pass up his daily shot of whiskey. And employment was just what Carl needed at that moment, considering he'd just walked away from not only school but the financially well-set life he'd always known with basically just the clothes on his back.

Soon after, he found the vacant castle nearby, took up residence, and began collecting things he'd need to live from his friends. With his candles, hibachi and free supply of running water, Carl lived off the land by snubbing the utility companies, at least during the warmer months. Winter always proved to be much more difficult for someone as anti-establishment as himself. If you planned on visiting him that time of year, you'd have to stay by the fireplace because the frost wasn't only on the outside windowpanes, it was also on the inside—not to mention the soot and smoke that filled the room from the long neglected chimney that fed that ancient fireplace. I guess you could say, at least, that he was lucky to have a forest full of shade trees so close by for kindling.

Winter wasn't the only problem he found with living off the land. Another was that he needed his music. To have that music, he needed electricity, which was only made possible when it was supplied by way of heavy-duty extension cords that ran down the hill through a neighbor's window and into his outlets in exchange for being invited to Carl's parties where this neighbor could indulge in unlimited drink and smoke while hopefully "getting lucky" with one of the many "loose hippie women" Carl seemed to know. I'm doubtful any of the women Carl knew were really "loose hippies," but from what Carl's told me, this seemed to be his neighbor's general impression of the Sixties, young American female, or at least his fantasy.

Carl had no phone, so I had to go get him on the days he was needed at the marina. Not having a car, I'd walk up to the Castle. I didn't really mind. I ran up the many circular steps two at a time, knocked on the door and waited, even though Carl would rather I, and everyone else, never knock and just enter. I was about to give up when he finally answered the door with wet hair and wearing faded, purple corduroy bells with a Hobie t-shirt, even though I knew he'd never surfed a day in his life.

"Nice threads!" I jokingly shielded my eyes with one hand from the brightness of the pants.

Looking down at them, he answered, "Some chick ripped off my jeans last night and decided to leave me hers."

"I wish some chick would rip off my jeans!"

"Hey man, if you don't like your pants, you can have these, we can trade," he offered seriously, while he studied the pants he'd been forced to wear and tugged at the waistband. "They're too fucking tight around the waist anyway."

"Uh, that's not what I meant. Forget it."

"Oh...I get it!" Carl just smiled at me and shook his head.

Sometimes I wanted to punch him out, him and his perfect hair. With hardly any effort on his part, those "rock star" looks would get him any girl he wanted, and he seemed completely oblivious to the fact. But even with those looks, evidently cool façade, and seven-night-a-week-one-night-stands, I knew as his close friend that in reality he was extremely insecure. Yet insecure as he was, he still managed to have a swagger in his walk, a false but brazen self-confidence that said to everyone, "Fuck you, I know who I am and what I want from this life," even though I'm sure—like most of us—he didn't really have a clue.

"I was just in the bathtub," he said smiling, while gesturing toward the spring on the side of the house. "Come in. You want some coffee?"

I followed him through the living room to the kitchen. Walking past the bookshelves, I couldn't help noticing his collection. Although there were some beaten up novels, some of them classic, the bulk of his selection seemed to pertain to pot. I couldn't help commenting on at least two of their titles.

"You've got quite an extensive library here," I pointed out. "*Homegrown Happiness* and *The Marijuana Consumer's and Dealer's Guide*?"

He cut me off before I could read more. "Yeah. My goal is to fill all four shelves."

"With all the same subject matter?"

"Ha ha! Maybe."

"Since when do you have a cat?" I noticed a large black one lying on the floor right under the spot where the sunlight came in through the windows.

"I don't. It comes and goes. I wish it would bring me some bread, but instead it just brings me dead things like mice and birds... sometimes rats."

"Nothing you can throw on the grill?"

He laughed. "You know I'm a vegetarian! What's up? Are my services needed today in the nautical world?"

"Yeah, but no rush. Whenever you're ready."

Within earshot, he stepped outside the kitchen door where he kept the hibachi. I watched him from behind, as he threw handfuls of coffee grinds into an old metal pan filled with water. He was the only one I knew that made coffee without a filter or measuring, but it came out perfect every time.

"You want some granola?" he asked, sniffing the milk carton while at the same time making a face. "I guess this is spent."

"No thanks but I will take some coffee." I sat down at the secondhand 1950s aluminum and Formica dinette set he'd acquired that, like so many other things, had found its way into his house by way of a friend or someone's curbside.

"Can you believe Martin Luther King got shot?" I said. "And all those cities rioting? Did you hear that down in Trenton they were hitting the police in the head with golf balls?"

"It's about time the fuzz got a taste of their own violent medicine. You know, the theory goes that you can't let the poor people, black or white, get smart because if they get too smart, they might revolt. The last thing the government wants are smart blacks like Martin Luther King. And they don't want the blacks and whites to come together and respect one another the way Dr. King wanted, either, because then the races would be equal, and the white man wouldn't rule anymore. What makes Big Brother and the fuzz happy is when there's riots and war. They have to keep the poor down and make sure they don't ever get the same education as the rich white kids. Keep them poor so the military looks like the only way out; why should the rich white kids sacrifice themselves? Too bad Abbie never got the Pentagon off the ground. I'd say it's about time the Alien Nation of America waved its freak flag and scared them shitless!"

"It sounds like you think the government had something to do with King's assassination," I asked, stunned but at the same time mesmerized once again by his consistently oddball logic.

"Man, who knows? I wouldn't be surprised. Sometimes I wonder if they had anything to do with J.F.K.'s assassination. If they could massacre hundreds of innocent civilians in cold blood, how hard could it be to knock off the president who is only one guy?

"What are you talking about?"

"Supposedly, the government is keeping it a secret that our soldiers killed a lot of Vietnamese recently...including women and children. All I know is it's a good thing I don't have an address if they should happen to come looking for me, because I refuse to fight in their war."

"Same here. Jane said she'll take us to Canada if we get drafted." I realized, the more I heard about the war, the more confused I was by our presence there.

Then he smiled to himself with that carnal grin that always made me wonder if Jane was also one of his many conquests. I hated that he depended on her whenever he needed a ride somewhere, but even more I hated the fact that she never refused. She drove me everywhere, too, and I don't know if she was conscious of it or not, or if it was just coincidence, but the weird thing about it was that Carl and I never seemed to be in her car at the same time. Even though she told me once that she had always found him extremely attractive from the moment he'd first arrived in town, she said she thought he was unfortunately too old for her. That's what she said, but I didn't believe her. I'd seen the way she'd hang on his every word like it was some kind of invaluable life lesson he was offering. And the way he'd let her borrow his albums for as long as she wanted when he wanted to "turn her on" to some new kind of music, then she'd go on for weeks at a time about how great that particular artist was, or like almost every other girl in town, she'd just happen to have an article of his clothing in her closet that she'd never part with. Now I was sorry I'd brought up her name and thought to quickly change the subject.

"Hey, I was in the Lookout the other day, and John was in there with Dunn and Hale. He was betting that for a thousand bucks he could jump off the bridge...and live!"

"That's some heavy shit, man. What's he smoking?"

"He said he'd have those guys wait for him underneath in a boat."

"What boat? Those guys don't have a boat."

"I know, right?"

"I hope they're not thinking of copping mine!" he added.

"Or mine."

"Speaking of boats, should we split? Hey, you sure you don't want to trade pants?"

"Hell, no! I'd have to say that purple is definitely your color."

"Get the hell out!" Carl said, as he laughed and pushed me out the door from behind.

***

As soon as we got to the marina, Carl quickly changed out of his purple pants and into a pair of denim cut-offs that he kept on his skiff. He then got out his radio and wasted no time fiddling around for WNEW. As we worked side by side, we talked about John and his crazy idea.

"He's just doing it for attention," Carl offered.

"Whose attention do you think he's trying to attract? I would have guessed his dad's, but he's long gone."

"You heard about the guy who tried that stunt right before the bridge was open to traffic?

He had the same idea, and said the same crazy thing John is saying now, that he'd survive the jump."

"No. What guy? When?"

"Some guy back in the Thirties, right after the bridge was built, decided to dive from 220 feet.

The dive went wrong in the last few seconds, and he landed on his back somehow. He wasn't the only victim; supposedly, he was the thirteenth, but the ones before him died from building the bridge."

Carl never cared much for John. I'd never even seen the two exchange more than a word between them. He had no patience for illiterate, apathetic people. John's lack of knowledge on U.S.

politics, which Carl felt came from John's refusal to read books or newspapers was what he didn't like. Carl said once, "You can't call the guy illiterate. We both know he can read." I never understood his disdain for John or how he came to that conclusion when he barely was around the guy.

I was a little more forgiving of John and his apathetic outlook on politics in this country and life in general. For one thing, it was obvious he didn't have much in the way of self-esteem. After witnessing firsthand for years the life John had to put up with at home, I was 100 percent sure that he had his father to blame for it. I knew he'd given up trying to please his dad years ago. I guess, at some point, John just gave up and stopped caring about everything, world politics included.

We were considered a rarity only because John went to Catholic school and I went to public.

Though we were the same age, in our town Catholic and public school kids didn't associate with each other, but since I'd grown up next door to John, I'd spend a lot of time at his house, as he did at mine.

As far back as I could remember, I think John's mom was my first crush. Of all my friends' mothers, Mrs. Kelly was the most attractive; with her shiny black hair and piercing blue eyes, she made me very nervous. Whenever I would call for John, she would always greet me at their front door with her thick Irish brogue that she never managed to lose in all the years she'd been in this country. I remember that she always kept a photo of "the only Irishman she'd ever loved; the love of her life" hanging by her calendar next to the refrigerator. She would look at it longingly every day. It was a photo of a very young—and according to a lot of other women at the time—very handsome, John F. Kennedy. She'd wink and whisper to me, "This is a secret between you and me, Henry. Don't ever tell Mr. Kelly, but I'd run away with the president in a second if given the chance."

She made the best iced tea, which took forever, but we didn't mind waiting. She'd also make sure John, Will and me never went hungry by seeing to it that we all had lunch or dinner if we were visiting, or money for the ice cream man or candy store if we were bored.

Mr. Kelly wasn't as welcoming to John's friends. Most of the time he would come home in a drunken rage from any one of the many taverns he'd had begun to frequent when he moved to town, as if suddenly possessed by alcohol himself. His tirades would begin in the driveway, and if we happened to hear him, John would become embarrassed and afraid. And even though his dad never allowed him to leave the house or yard, unless it was for school, John would always suggest that we leave his house as soon as possible. I'd feel sorry for leaving Mrs. Kelly there all alone, but she was used to it after so many years, I guess. From what John told me, his father was never easy to live with, even before he took up drinking.

On those infernal, eternal summer afternoons, we'd usually end up walking to the local candy store where grumpy old Mr. Dempsey would be sitting behind the counter reminding us to "Hurry up, get what you're getting and get out! There's no loitering allowed!" Since I was pretty young at the time, I remember thinking how could I be "loitering" if I didn't even know what the word meant?

I also recall being too afraid to ask Mr. Dempsey exactly what "loitering" was for fear of getting yelled at some more, so I waited until I got home to ask. His demeanor never changed, day after day, year after year. It left me wondering why a man with that kind of disposition chose to own a business that was frequented by kids—a candy store, no less!

We'd not only buy candy but also packs of baseball cards with horrible-tasting, powdered gum inside, Spalding balls that would soon go flat from the daily abuse they took, and Coke in green glass bottles, each with a different state stamped on its bottom. Once, we spent an entire summer trying to collect all fifty states; we came pretty close.

Some days, we'd go down to the marina with our nets and catch crabs, only to let them go again, because not only were they too ugly and scary-looking to eat, but we also felt sorry for them.

Then we'd usually make it home every afternoon just in time for the Good Humor man. Dressed in his weird white uniform—the creepy kind actors wore when they were portraying insane asylum workers in those old movies—he would always leave an open Dixie cup inside the gate for Fritz. We usually would know when he was coming because Fritz would start to bark long before we could hear his bell. Like most dogs, he was able to tell the difference between one engine's sound and another's, so once it became familiar to him, he could hear the truck from miles away.

As we hit our teens, John and I began to grow apart. It seemed like it happened overnight that he'd become more drawn to his Catholic school friends and me to my public school ones. Our houses—once so familiar to each of us—suddenly, and without any discussion between our parents or ourselves, seemed off limits to one another. If we happened to run into each other on the street, there wasn't even time for brief conversation anymore; we'd just barely wave hello in passing.

Later on came the nights that I'd be forced awake by the color red flashing on and off that, even with my eyes closed, I could still see. Most of the time, I couldn't tell if the police were there for Mr. Kelly, or John, or both. I'd usually wake up and look through the blinds only to find the patrol car with its flashing lights and blaring siren, a signal that something was going on at the Kelly's house...again. But that one night it was different. That time it was ambulance lights that woke me, and the strange thing about it was there had been no warning siren. What usually preceded the siren in the past could have been anything from screeching brakes, crunching metal, shattering glass—since Mr. Kelly would usually end up hitting someone's parked car with his own, or a combination of all three sounds followed by the Kellys screaming at each other. But that night I didn't remember being awakened by any noise and was sure I hadn't slept through it since no one in my house seemed to have woken up either. Yet through the flashing red blinds I could see people gathering in the street. Up until that day I didn't know what a body bag was since I'd never seen one. Now I knew. That's how they brought Mr. Kelly out. I could barely see the outlines of Mrs. Kelly and John, along with the neighbors: everyone silent, like frozen statues caught in the rhythmic red lights, as she stood with her arm around him and faced the ambulance when Mr. Kelly was placed inside.

***

Unlike most of us, even though Carl lived in town now, he didn't grow up in Pleasant Valley. His "Castle" on the hill seemed like the perfect place for him to look down on the town, as he surveyed each one of us. An avid reader of American politics and its effects on the world, he believed the United States screwed with many of the countries in the world for whatever we could pillage and plunder to get at their natural resources for our own monetary gain, resources that the United States assumed was our own for the taking without ever having regard for the welfare of the citizens of those countries. He also felt there were a lot of small-minded people in town who were in their own little world and didn't care that much for politics or anything else that went on outside Pleasant Valley. Then again, he knew there were those in town that did care, and it didn't matter to him if they were against his views and planned to vote for Nixon in November or were for the War. All that mattered to Carl was that some chose to break free from their little world and took the time to bother to form their own opinions, whether he agreed with those opinions or not.

In a way he was right: We were in our own little world. How could we not be? It seemed unavoidable. I was beginning to think that maybe there really was something to this whole "solar deprivation" theory. Maybe the *Metropolitan Times* was right: Less sun did seem to equal more booze and drugs when it came to this place. I knew I felt it, that oppressive feeling of being stuck in a hole at the bottom of a towering wall of stone that closed us off from the rest of the world, where the only escape was uphill north or south, or by way of the river.

With a barricade of bluestone behind us, that sound itself couldn't even escape, everything would come bouncing back in echoes: echoes from the aluminum mill, amusement park, emergency vehicle sirens, revving of car engines, even thunder. The only place that didn't feel oppressive was out on the river in a boat far away from the suffocating cliffs that felt like they might swallow us up if we turned our backs for even a second. Along with that feeling came apathy and the negative reputation we couldn't shake for being a blue-collar town that loved to fight. Most residents from other towns would refuse to come down to Pleasant Valley, as if visiting our town was like entering the depths of hell. It was far from fiery hell. Winters were the worst since we'd lose the sun even earlier than the towns above us, making it so cold and dark that it was actually painful.

***

I looked over at Carl working beside me, as he was humming along to the radio. "I heard John is going to go through with his stunt. He's decided to do it on the Fourth."

"Well then, he'll have quite an audience," Carl added, sarcastically.

Every Fourth of July there was a picnic in the Veteran's Field with a decent fireworks display that was set off from barges out on the river. It was first come, first served for the tables and cookers that rested under a crescent of ancient weeping willows. There were free-flowing kegs, plus a local band that covered a lot of Sixties garage band music like the Blues Magoos, Leaves, Standells, and even some Yardbirds. The older folks didn't care much for the music; it was always the kegs that closed the generation gap since it was hard to find a teetotaler—man or woman, young or old—in our town.

Dirty Water

C arl had reminded me when my eighteenth birthday finally arrived that I'd already experienced most rites of passage for someone my age: I'd driven a car, consumed alcohol, and smoked cigarettes.

Sometimes I'd even smoke the kind with tobacco. The only thing left, he surmised, was losing my virginity. I admit though, I was embarrassed he knew my situation and actually confronted me about it.

I guess my shyness was obvious when it came to girls.

To celebrate my birthday, my parents had planned a day out on my dad's boat. Our first stop would be the Dreikanter, a New York waterfront restaurant, for lunch and drinks. After lunch, we'd drop anchor close to shore at Croton to swim and drink some more.

Like Lenny, my dad had no reservations about my underage drinking, as long as it wasn't hard liquor, since his own dad, my grandfather, would tell him when he was at an age much younger than I was to drink the beer and save the ginger ale for the adult's mixed drinks whenever my parents would entertain. So today I'd finally be legally old enough to try my first Tom Collins, Sloe Gin Fizz, or Rye and Ginger. And if I couldn't decide between them, then maybe I'd have one of each.

Although my dad's boat actually did have a cabin with a bathroom, or "head," a galley, and an area for dining—which could be converted into beds by taking down the table—you could say the cabin cruiser was a little on the small side.

He always kept a church key in the galley that was tied to the wall by a rope for opening the Budweiser kept in the cooler. The cooler also was kept there so it was out of sight should the Coast Guard decide to come on board for a surprise visit, which they would do randomly, and was always something we hoped to avoid.

There were nine of us: mom, dad, Will, Steven, Jane, Carl, Ike, my grandfather and myself; too many according to Coast Guard standards, especially since we only had six life jackets. Steven had brought along a transistor radio that would only play AM but was better than nothing. As we left the marina, the Monkees were singing, "Pleasant Valley Sunday." Although the "status symbol-land" part of the song didn't apply, I thought it was a real coincidence for it to actually be Sunday and in Pleasant Valley. We could even smell the "charcoal burning everywhere" from the barbeque pits onshore at Palisades Interstate Park. The weather was perfect; the sky cloudless against the backdrop of treetops shimmered on lush, verdant cliffs. It wasn't quite summer yet, but it felt and smelled like it.

To keep Will from getting bored, Mom had brought stale bread for him to throw to the sea gulls, and it wasn't long before we had a large flock following us, screaming and fighting one another as they would each dive for the bread.

At the stern, the sound of the engine and rush of water as the boat maneuvered through other boats' wakes made hearing the radio or even our conversation impossible, so Carl, Jane, Steven and I went up on deck to be able to hear ourselves and the music. At my dad's instruction, we waved to the right or left, alerting him which way to go to avoid running over large pieces of driftwood. We'd also wave—as was customary on the Hudson—to boaters as they passed, and they would wave back, my dad steering into their wakes if they went by us too quickly.

As we pulled up to the Dreikanter's private dock for restaurant patrons, Will quickly hopped off and to our surprise tied us up. Without our knowledge, Carl had been successful in not only teaching Will the difference between a bow line and a bowline, but also how to tie all different kinds of nautical knots. We were very impressed that in just a matter of weeks, Will had learned to tie a buntline hitch, bowline and clove hitch. However, Carl couldn't believe it when we told him that Will still wasn't able to tie his shoes. Carl then decided to let me know in private that we had two goals that summer: besides seeing to it personally that Will would be able to tie his shoes, he would devise a plan with someone of the opposite sex, preferably experienced, to help change my virgin status. He'd never let me live it down since that day I saw him wearing those purple pants, when I confessed that I wished some "chick," any "chick," would rip off mine. I was sorry I'd ever opened my mouth.

The inside of the restaurant looked like an old hunting lodge with stiff white linen napkins perched like tiny tents on plates while frozen pats of butter sat resting in a bowl of ice. Cigarette smoke hung close to the ceiling and permeated everything in the place, including the napkins and the butter.

The hunting lodge atmosphere included moose and deer heads and even a wild boar's head, all mounted on the walls. Also, in a shadowbox-type frame on one wall was some kind of animal's paw with a description of how the hunter obtained it, written years ago from the looks of the faded ink on yellowed paper.

I sensed that it bothered Will that there were animal heads on the walls and that the lobster our mom had ordered also still had its head when it was brought to our table. To be on the safe side, he ordered his usual cheeseburger and seemed proud of his choice after informing us that cheeseburgers don't have heads. I was waiting for Carl, the strict vegetarian, to say otherwise, so I quickly shot him a wide-eyed warning glance. Will also didn't like the idea that some of our drinks came with tiny umbrellas yet his Shirley Temple didn't. Jane offered him hers, but he wouldn't take it, letting the waiter know he needed to have one of his own.

After lunch we headed to Croton, dad letting Will navigate. Slightly buzzed, the four of us decided to go up on deck again, taking turns one at a time, alerting my dad and Will to large pieces of wood, while the rest of us took in some sun. As Carl stretched out on the right side of the deck, tan and shirtless in his denim cut-offs, Steven and I stretched out on the left, also shirtless but anemic-looking and in uninspiring swim trunks. All the while, Jane was in the middle not hiding the fact that she was fervently taking in the seemingly more attractive view on her right.

We found a place offshore and dropped anchor. Then each of us, including Will, decided to take turns jumping off the deck: Our goal would be trying to land in the center of an inner tube that was tied to the bow.

I didn't let on that I was a little squeamish. Even though Croton seemed cleaner and had actual sand at the bottom rather than the muck that was at the river bottom off Pleasant Valley's beaches, there was still the chance of bumping into something undesirable. While boating, some of my dad's friends had said on occasion they'd seen body parts and dead dogs floating past them. I was yet to see anything like that, but all the same I kept a vigilant watch, at least on the surface of the water. I also wanted to be able to open my eyes underwater and be forewarned about what I might chance bumping into, but it didn't matter if you opened your eyes under the Hudson; it was so dense and opaque that you couldn't even see your own body parts in front of your face, much less ones that might happen to float past.

As we got ready to leave Croton, we pulled up anchor and started the engine. We were even more buzzed at that point, since we did a pretty good job emptying the cooler. None of us chose to sit up near the hatch for fear of falling off. Instead, we sat in the tiny cabin playing cards. Thankfully, because of Carl's sage advice, I had stuck to one kind of mixed drink at the restaurant instead of trying many, although mixing beer and sun for the rest of the afternoon didn't really help. Knowing he had to get us all home safely, my dad was the only one who had curbed his drinking.

Things were pretty uneventful for the first half-hour of our trip back home, and then...WHAM!

It was like we'd struck an invisible boat head on. My dad's boat came to an abrupt halt, and there was this terrible grinding mechanical sound, then silence; the boat had stalled. Through all this, the table we sat at had broken free from the wall, while I watched through the cabin door as Will and my mom got thrown off their feet. My dad tried to start the boat again: once, twice, three times. It was like a feeble car engine hopelessly trying to turn over. None of us had realized the serious situation we were in until we saw dark water rapidly entering the cabin through the floorboards. Where we sat, the silence was soon interrupted by the bilge pump going on automatically as the boat desperately tried to save itself from going under.

"We hit something, and I'm afraid whatever it is, it's pretty big!" my dad yelled to us. He told me to quickly remove the American flag from its pole on the stern, and start waving it upside down at the passing boats to show that we were in distress. My first thought was that he'd lost his mind. In all my years of working at the marina and being around boats, I had no experience in what I should do if there was a disaster that involved any watercraft bigger than my rowboat. But waving a flag upside down seemed like a silly and senseless thing to do. I did as he asked anyway, and as I removed the flag from its holder, I stood on the cushioned seat at the stern and began waving it. My dad then attempted to light the flares, which had gotten wet since they were stored inside the cabin seats.

The boats that passed us were few and far between. The water was coming in fast. The sun would be going down which meant that if we weren't rescued soon, there was a good chance that no one would see us and we'd be hit again, only this time from above the water. Continuing to hold the pole so that the flag was at its bottom, I frantically waved at each boat as they passed. In the meantime, dad was still having no luck lighting the flares.

My mom went from "tipsy," as she referred to her state when we left the restaurant, to panic-stricken in a matter of seconds when she got out the life jackets and was reminded that not only were we in the middle of the river where it was very deep, but that there were only six. With Will, my mom and Jane, that meant there'd be only three left. Carl and I argued with my grandfather and Ike for them to take two of the life jackets. My dad reminded us that there was no time for arguing. Stubborn, the four of us went without. Besides waving, we were all screaming for help. Most of the boaters that passed never saw us, and the ones that saw us from a distance must have thought we were just being friendly since they'd only wave back and continue on their way. I had never seen Will so afraid, as my mom helped him into his life jacket, and he clutched onto his little plastic statue for dear life.

All of a sudden, Steven noticed that a much larger cabin cruiser than my dad's that had just passed us moments ago, was actually turning around and seemed to be headed right for us. Within what seemed like seconds, they had their stern facing the bow of our boat. My dad yelled to the kind stranger that we hit something big, and we were going down fast.

"I could see that you were listing badly—they say there's an uncharted sunken barge out here; I don't think you're the first to hit it!" the man yelled back. "Let's get everyone off your boat as quickly as possible, and I'll tie you up behind us. There's a marina not far from here. I don't think you'll be able to make it any farther than that without your boat going under. We'll go kind of fast to keep as much new water from coming into it as possible."

Dad decided he'd stay on our boat. He dumped the ice from the cooler and would use it to bail out as much water as he could while the boat was moving. Carl and I offered to stay with him, but he said, "No!" then ordered all of us to go through the cabin, women and Will first, so we could hoist them from behind through the deck hatch, the deck being the most direct way to reach the boat that was rescuing us.

It took the accident to sober us all up quickly. Jane, the first in line and the first to enter the eerily dark, lifeless cabin, had stopped suddenly and froze with everyone else behind her. Terrified, she refused to move when she stepped on the floor, and it started to fall through. Seeing the dark water and hearing the bilge pump's futile efforts directly beneath her feet made her unable to go forward. She had never given any thought to the bottomless depth of the river until now. She had always considered herself a good swimmer, but it was another thing to be stuck inside the cabin of a boat that was sinking fast into what looked like an unfathomable void.

My dad yelled at her through the cabin door, one of the few times in my life that I'd ever heard him raise his voice. "Go! Move!

Now!"

"I can't! I can't!" she cried, as she stood paralyzed and on the verge of tears with the long line of us waiting behind her. "The floor is gone!"

I looked down at my feet and realized she was right: the floor was sinking and almost completely gone. We had to balance with our arms resting on the seats to keep from falling through, while our feet dangled in the black, foreboding water. From the stern, my dad yelled at us again through the cabin door opening not to worry about the floor, and to get up and walk on the seats.

With our boat already tied to the other boat, Jane finally conquered her fears and climbed through the hatch without much help from us. My mom and Will followed. It took myself, Carl and Ike to get my grandfather through. If it had taken any more time, we feared we would have had no choice but to leave him with my dad, because if the boat had remained stationary for much longer, it would have become completely submerged, possibly pulling the other boat under with it.

The second we got everyone on board the rescuing boat, it took off for the closest marina going at a pretty fast pace. We all kept our eyes on my dad's boat tied behind us, hoping he would be safe, all the while wondering why the sunken barge had been left uncharted, and knowing even before our boat had been put on a lift that it was totaled.

Pictures of Matchstick Men

I was drifting off to sleep when I heard something hit my bedroom window. The familiar sound forced me to get up and look out at the back yard, where I saw John sitting on our well cover, smoking a cigarette and flinging pebbles at the panes.

"Just like old times!" he yelled up at me as quietly as he could, considering the late hour. He was referring to when we were both younger, and he'd signal me late at night to sneak out of the house. Back then we'd go down to the marina, the Veteran's Field or the Seatrain dock with a bottle of whatever he'd stolen from his father's stash. We'd sit and talk for hours about our future hopes and dreams even though the whole time I'd hardly drink and was always afraid my parents would wake and worry if they found me gone.

"Can you hang out for a little while? I need to talk to someone."

"Sure. I'll be right there," I answered awkwardly, thinking how out of character this was for him to approach me, especially now that so much time had passed since we were friends. When I got outside, he smiled, opened his jacket and flashed a cheap bottle of wine.

"You feel like walking down to Seatrain?" he asked.

Seatrain was a platform dock where containers were loaded from cargo ships onto the back of truck cabs. Not just a loading dock, but also a place where out of town drivers, tired of their cars and wanting new ones, would purposely lose their rides to the river so they could claim they were stolen and collect the insurance money. The cops finally got wise, though when portions of the vehicle graveyard starting rising out of the mud at low tide.

As we walked there he asked me what I planned to do with myself and if I would be moving away, since he knew I had just graduated. Being a year older, he'd graduated the year before and as far as I could tell, just like me, he really didn't seem to have a plan for himself either.

We walked out to the end of the platform and sat, letting our legs dangle over the side. Through the darkness I pointed out the hulks of rusting relics that rose out of the river water in places. He unscrewed the wine and passed it to me. The cheap wine reminded me of what damp, dirty socks that had spent weeks at the bottom of a laundry hamper might taste like.

"What's it all about?" he asked.

"What do you mean?"

"Life, this town. We get up every day and go through the same motions, never getting anywhere, only to grow old and die. I don't want to get old. And I want to leave here, see places.

Most of the time I feel like I'm suffocating, drowning in the shadows. Don't you ever feel like that?"

"Yeah, sometimes," I answered. "I feel it more in winter." I wanted to be sympathetic and show John I related since he seemed so vulnerable and most of all lonely.

I cleared my throat and summoned up the courage to ask him if he was still going through with what I'd heard him say at the Lookout, half expecting Dunn and Hale to be hiding in the dark somewhere, ready to jump out and pummel me to death.

"I heard what you said at Lenny's."

"What did I say?"

"That you were planning to jump off the bridge for a thousand bucks."

We both looked in the bridge's direction, as I waited for him to answer. After a long pause, he said, "Do you think I can do it?"

"Are you trying to kill yourself?"

With a heavy sigh, he quickly jumped to his feet, saying, "I gotta take a piss."

I watched him walk off to the side of the brick building. I heard him urinating against the concrete, then the sound of shattering glass as he flung the empty wine bottle against the wall.

We both agreed to head home since the wine was gone. When we got there, I realized that he'd never answered my question.

He reached out to shake my hand, while he pulled me close to hug me with his free arm. "If I don't see you later, I'm really sorry, man."

I didn't know what he meant by that. He stepped back away from me and I swore that I saw his eyes tearing up. I wanted to ask him exactly what he was apologizing for, but without saying anything else, he turned and went into his house.

***

I never told anyone that John and I had hung out just days before. Then the Fourth arrived, and I was one of the many pathetic witnesses standing on shore, waiting to watch him jump from the bridge. For some reason, no one in the audience was much older than myself. Even Lenny, who threatened to warn Mrs. Kelly of the stunt, wasn't there.

John had dressed all in black like some cat burglar in the hopes of making himself invisible to passing motorists or Port Authority Police who might otherwise see him and possibly stop to try and discourage what, in their eyes, could only be a suicide victim. High above the Hudson, with one foot in New Jersey and the other in New York, he'd hurl his extremely inebriated self over the railing on the naive notion that drunk people were so relaxed they could never get hurt. He was much more concerned with the muck he'd come in contact with as his feet touched the bottom of the river than the fact that the force of the fall would actually cause his feet to end up getting shoved into his ribcage, causing his ribs to become like knives slicing through his organs as they rebounded inside him.

Carl had wanted no part of watching John's circus act, so Steven, Jane and I left him at the picnic, at his request, by the only remaining, yet to be emptied keg. We followed the tree-lined dirt road that ran parallel to the river until we came to the bridge. A large group already was assembled there. It was very dark. The only illumination other than the skyline was from the bridge itself and some fireworks in the distance. Dunn and Hale had parked their van under the bridge on a boat ramp.

They knew better than to keep the headlights on for any length of time, since that was one area the police patrolled frequently because that dark little road ran parallel to Old River Road, a road often used by a lot of out-of-towners to run drugs. Access to the bridge and tunnel from the road made it a quick way to escape police across state lines.

A bunch of us stood on the riverbank. From the beach below we could barely see John's tiny silhouette on the bridge's upper deck. Worried, we all secretly hoped he wouldn't follow through with it, yet none of us had tried to stop him. None of us could at that point; it was too late. In the middle of the river, Dunn and Hale sat waiting in the boat. Dunn held a flashlight, signaling John to show their location by pointing it up at him and flashing it on and off intermittently. We waited and waited for what seemed like a very long time, then without any warning, he fell screaming, feet first, into the blackness. It was an eerie, fearless scream like he was on some sort of amusement park ride.

Then he hit the water like it was concrete, broke through it, and was gone from sight. First, there was just shock and silence among us, interrupted only by the occasional explosion of fireworks in the distance.

What soon followed was a frantic commotion from those of us on shore, as Dunn and Hale rowed in circles trying to locate him with the current only making matters worse. It took a while for them to find him, Dunn being cautious not to overuse the flashlight and attract the police. He had fallen far from where they expected him to land, closer to the New York side, by Jeffrey's Hook. The little antique lighthouse, no longer in operation was awkward and out of place, having been forced to stand for decades beneath the monstrous steel structure of a bridge. It was like some slight, snuffed out candle now, useless and irrelevant since it could no longer offer light to guide Dunn and Hale to him.

When he surfaced and they pulled him like a broken doll into the boat, they screamed to us on shore that he was still alive. But from where we were standing, he appeared lifeless, motionless and speechless; he might as well have been dead. And then, Steven pointed to the boat, "Hey, isn't that your...?" I couldn't believe my eyes! The whole experience of watching John jump was weird enough, but seeing him being put into my boat was even weirder! I had to get a closer look just to be certain, and sure enough, to my horror, I noticed the little aluminum boat had the same registration number that I knew so well. Was that what John meant when he apologized the other night, that he was sorry he'd be stealing my boat?

I had to wonder now that if he died as a result of the jump, would Dunn and Hale be accessories to murder? Would I, since it was my boat they were using? Was it just a matter of time before the police came knocking at my door? But this was such a small town where nothing ever happened. Would the cops even know what to do? And since he technically fell in another state, would there be other police involved, too, besides Pleasant Valley, like the New York City or Port Authority police?

I ran to the boat ramp to confront Dunn and Hale. I think, for the first time in my life, my usual nonviolent nature had suddenly faded. I screamed "Who said you pricks could steal my boat?!" They ignored me and everyone else, as they got into the van. I ran up alongside them and pounded on the driver's side window with my fist. "Hey! I'm talking to you!"

Headlights off, they sped away quickly. Then a few feet in front of me on the sand I saw what looked like a rumpled pile of clothes. It took me a second to realize they'd left John behind, lying on the beach. Where were they going? Did these guys really expect a different outcome, like maybe him being fine afterwards, just a little wet, and the three of them all going out for drinks, John's treat?

Even if the police were told the truth—that he was stupid enough to jump on a bet—it was just too bizarre to be believed. The other truth—an awful one that we would all have to live with for the rest of our lives—was that after John jumped and they pulled him from the water, Dunn and Hale rowed the boat to shore, took him out and left him lying on the beach unconscious. And then all of us—equally as spineless—would run like cowards and leave him there to die all alone.

I realized I needed to do something about John. Terrified that I'd be implicated in the crime, I needed something to do about the boat, too. I couldn't think straight, but there was no time to think. At that moment, I wanted to get in the boat and row it back to the marina, but I noticed Dunn and Hale hadn't secured it, and it had already drifted way out of reach.

Everyone had fled the scene quickly, fearing the police might show up at any minute, but Steven, Jane and I couldn't leave him there to die; we also couldn't stick around. He looked like a broken marionette lying there on his back with his legs all mangled and twisted. I checked and found he had a faint pulse. We turned him on his side in case he had swallowed a lot of water. None of us knew CPR. I told him we were going to get help. Staring up at nothing, he didn't respond. The best idea we came up with was to walk a half mile to the closest payphone and make an anonymous call to the police alerting them to the location of the body of an unconscious man we found lying on the beach under the bridge, a man that all of us pretended not to know.

***

The three of us were too nervous and wound up to sleep. I regretted watching the whole horrendous stunt, but mostly I regretted not being the one who tried to stop it. I must have went over the scene a million times in my head about what it must have been like for John, what he saw and what he felt. I imagined him after he'd finally surfaced, waiting silently as he floated in the cold, wet darkness, putting all his faith and trust into two guys with a flashlight and a boat. Then, seeing flashes of light exploding above him, he'd probably remember they were fireworks, he'd remember it was the Fourth, as he fought to stay conscious, battling not only fierce pain but the current that would attempt to move him quickly downriver, when the cold, hostile water might start to play tricks on his mind. He'd hear someone calling his name in the distance but no matter how hard he'd try, he'd be unable to answer, unable to move.

We decided to walk back to the Veteran's Field to find Carl and tell him that John had gone through with it. And we were sure that if John wasn't dead already, he would be soon. As we left the bridge area, we could already hear the sirens coming closer. I had called the Pleasant Valley Police just moments earlier; they really didn't really have far to travel since the town was so small.

When we got to the Veteran's Field, Carl was nowhere to be found, just a few old guys hanging around, draining the last keg. We decided to walk to the Castle and let him know John jumped. Even though the Castle sat overlooking the river it was adjacent to the bridge path where we'd just left John to die.

As we were climbing the stone steps to his house—the three of us well hidden from the trees all around us—we could see the ambulance and police cars below, one following the other, as they raced to the entrance of the dirt road we had just fled from. I prayed to myself that he'd hang on, that there'd be something they could do for him, but I knew that he'd need a miracle.

When we got to Carl's front door, we could see the dim flicker of candlelight through the windows. He definitely wasn't alone; he had the radio on, and we could hear a girl's voice.

"Maybe this isn't a good time." Jane offered.

"Hey, this is important—I think he should know what happened tonight," I answered. Then I knocked hard on his front door to alert him that we were there. I yelled, "Carl, it's us!"

He clearly didn't hear us because they went on talking. I tried the doorknob, and the door opened. We decided to enter, since he told us to never bother knocking anyway.

"I don't know about this," Jane said.

"If he doesn't want anyone just walking in then he should lock his door." We slowly followed the music to the kitchen. He was sitting at the dinette table with an attractive young girl on his lap, a girl I didn't recognize. He was whispering in her ear, and she was giggling. The volume on his battery-operated radio was turned up high, while candlelight danced to the music.

"Carl!" I yelled again, as I waved from the kitchen doorway,

Steven and Jane behind me.

When he saw us, Jane in particular, for some reason, he suddenly jumped up from his chair causing the girl to slide off his lap onto the floor. Both he and the girl looked extremely high. I still couldn't figure out why Jane had this effect on him. The guilt he reflected was almost as if she were his mom entering the room, and had just showed her disapproval at catching him alone with a girl.

"What's up, guys?" Helping the girl off the floor but not apologizing for putting her there, he introduced her by saying, "This is Adelaide...Adelaide Leary, a friend of mine from the city.

Steven and I said hello. Jane didn't.

"Well, he went through with it," I said.

"Damn! Is he alive?" Carl asked, then turned to the girl to explain the whole plan behind the spectacle we had all witnessed earlier without him.

"Barely. It doesn't look like he'll make it. Fucking Dunn and Hale left him on the beach and drove off. Everyone else booked, too. We decided to call the police."

Carl turned his radio down. "Which police? Pleasant Valley?"

"Yeah," Steven said. "We couldn't just leave him there. We didn't give our names, though."

Then I added, "Remember when we were talking about how those guys didn't have a boat, and we were hoping they didn't steal one of ours?" Carl looked afraid that I was going to say that they stole his boat. "Well, they took mine.

"Steven was the one who noticed that the boat had Henry's registration number." Jane added.

"Where is it now?" Carl asked.

"Gone...too far out in the river to get it back. I feel like, for that reason alone, I'm going to be dragged into this," I said, unable to stop myself from shaking.

Carl got out some more glasses and poured us some of the wine he and the girl had already been drinking. The girl then got up, kissed Carl on the cheek and said she should probably be leaving. Jane—who, up until that point, had been silent the whole time—visibly brightened and moved quickly to the dinette chair closest to Carl.

"You'll just have to tell the truth, that the boat was stolen," Carl said.

"What proof do I have?"

"Drink...don't think about it for now. If and when the time comes, we'll all vouch for you that they took it."

"Thanks!" I could feel the effect of the wine finally starting to calm me down.

Later that night as I got into bed, I looked through my window at the Kelly's house and realized that John would probably never be coming back home...or so, I thought.

***

Besides the eerie silence that had fallen over the town since John's jump, the rain had also been falling...nonstop. The three of us were not only broke but bored as hell. We'd watched so many episodes of *Dark Shadows* and *Get Smart* for days that we were tired of it. Anything to take our minds off John, if only for a while, but it didn't work. It seemed nothing would. We sat watching the relentless rain as it whipped at the windowpanes of Steven and Jane's waterfront home. Only late afternoon, yet the sky was dark as night already.

When the rain seemed to let up, for lack of anything better to do Steven suggested we take a walk down to the Veteran's Field to set off some bottle rockets and other small fireworks that he found left over from the Fourth. At first, we felt guilty lighting them, knowing they would echo off the cliffs, disturbing the uncomfortable hush that had fallen over the town since John's accident, but we soon learned that we found a certain release or solace in it. Even though they seemed to crack the air with indifference or disrespect, that was not our intention. With him in the hospital and barely clinging to life, we were in no way celebrating his unfortunate accident.

When they were all used up, we sat on a picnic table staring blankly at the river and the skyline, all the while ignoring the bridge like some great, gray, slumbering monster to our left in the distance. The night air felt damp from all the rain that had fallen in the past three days. The table where we sat was under a willow tree whose branches were heavy with water and thought nothing of spraying us whenever the wind blew.

Breaking the silence I said, "I'm in deep shit if my dad or grandfather—or even worse the police—find out what that boat was used for."

Jane, her usual procrastinating self, put her arm around me. "Don't worry about today what you can worry about tomorrow."

"But where did it go? Where is it now? And why couldn't those guys have left it close to shore?" The three of us didn't know if we were shivering from being cold or from the menacing presence of the bridge, even though we refused to look in its direction. "I'm wet and cold, and these mosquitoes are starting to get to me," Steven said. "I'm leaving. I'll catch up with you guys later."

Jane and I decided to stay a little longer and talk. Then we took the shortcut home that went past the old trolley tracks that were carved into the Palisades almost a century ago and wound their way 200 feet up to the top of the cliffs. The trolleys were long gone, but the amusement park they had served was still there at the top, as it had been since 1898. Besides rides and a giant pool, at one time it even had its own freak show—not to be confused with Carl, or those like him who liked to refer to themselves as one in the same. I had seen the show once years ago, and once was enough for me.

There was the "Elephant Lady," whose skin was supposed to resemble her namesake, striking a pose with her lonesome, despondent smile offered for everyone to gawk and whisper, the farm animals with multiple limbs, and the two-headed fetus in a jar. And those were just three of the many bizarre attractions.

In summer, the park was so brightly lit that the light pollution blocked out many of the stars.

Only in winter when the park was closed could you look up and see a clear sky. But when summer came, just looking up and seeing the Ferris wheel and hearing the screams of those who rode the rickety wooden roller coaster as they echoed off the cliffs was somehow better than in winter when the sky was filled with stars but the park was still.

The kids from Pleasant Valley always knew how to sneak in the park for free. We'd climb the cliffs in the woods and come out behind the sound stage where live music was being performed by groups like the Rascals or The Lovin' Spoonful. Jane had always hoped she'd bump into John Sebastian...literally. If you were lucky enough to get behind the stage without being noticed by security, all you had to do was walk quickly and confidently like you knew which direction you were going, and you'd be inside the park for free: past the giant saltwater swimming pool with its one-and-a-half million gallons courtesy of the Hudson River below; past the three-foot deep, trucked-in-sand "beach" acquired from the Atlantic coastline; past the bathhouse lockers, where the cologne of choice those days seemed to be Coppertone; past the stands where vinegar fries were cooked consistently perfect every time; past the concession stand lined with rows of glass bowls filled with colored water and goldfish (the object of the game was to get a ping pong ball in any bowl on the first try, which I'm sure, literally scared most of the fish to death, and was the reason that they were usually dead by the time you got them home); past rides like the Matterhorn, where the rider could pretend to escape the summer heat and be taken to a wintry, faraway place, past the giant mansion of a fun house and its many hidden rooms with moving floors and walls; and finally, past the sounds of the top 40 blaring over popping air rifles and wooden prize wheels spinning out someone's luck for the day.

The road that ran by the trolley tracks was the quickest way home. The hour was late, which meant the amusement park above was already closed. It was so quiet that we could hear the traffic light changing as we approached it.

Jane said in a hushed voice, "Don't look now, but here comes trouble."

"Damn!" I said. "It's Dunn and Hale, and they both look shitfaced."

If Dunn was drunk, you knew there'd always be some sort of

confrontation. Once, during a one-sided fistfight at a factory initiation with a crowd cheering him on—and John in the background quietly watching, as usual—Dunn had managed to knock a guy's eye out of its socket. The guy's displaced eye, which was dangling on his cheek, only caused the crowd to yell for more. After witnessing that, I remember being in a corner and having the strong urge to vomit, while Dunn watched me, the whole time laughing at me, as if he was proud of what he'd done.

When it came to Dunn and Hale together, neither one was the leader, and I don't think either one was smarter than the other, but they could both be just as combative as they were clueless.

"Hey, river rats, where's the party?" Dunn said to us, as he grabbed me by the front of my shirt.

When I tried to pull away, he gave me a shot in my right eye, a sucker punch that I never saw coming.

I could have remained standing, but being the cowardly, inexperienced fighter that I was, I chose to pretend that I was knocked out cold, or better yet, dead. Except for the pain I felt from the punch, I couldn't help imagining that I was one of those silent film stars who had probably stood in this exact spot, on those very same tracks so long ago, rehearsing some movie scene in the days when our town was Hollywood. But we weren't in costumes, and I sure as hell wasn't standing. Lying face down, I made sure I kept my eyes closed. Kneeling beside me, I heard Jane question Dunn angrily and without an ounce of fear, saying, "What did you do that for?"

His asinine reply was that if John died, it would be my fault. He then yelled for Hale to come on, they were leaving. As Jane helped me to my feet, even though I'd suddenly become very nauseous, and I could feel my eye quickly swelling closed, I thanked God that at least it was still in its socket.

I Had Too Much to Dream Last Night

The summer air hung over the city skyline like an oversized, dirty orange bedsheet. From across the room, I could see through my window the violet streetlamps of the West Side Highway twinkling across the river. It was 2 a.m., and I lay in bed timing the three minutes between every flight path of every plane leaving Newark, La Guardia and Kennedy. Trying to force sleep, I visualized the planes as sheep with engines, but sheep had never worked for me in the past. Forget motorized sheep I thought, any kind of breeze would have been a help. Sleeping with just a thin blanket was even too much. That was the one thing about New Jersey in the summer, especially after it rained; it would get so humid sometimes that it could feel almost like a jungle. The carpeting would even feel wet from all the moisture in the air, and the wood on the windows and doors swelled so much, they were hard to open and close. No matter that both windows were open, as there was no way to escape the oppressive heat.

For some reason, I felt drawn to the window on the opposite side of my room. I decided to get out of bed and take a look outside. My eyes traveled downward directly under that window to the ground below, where I was sure that I definitely saw what appeared to be someone sitting on the well cover in our backyard. With his head down, from what I could see, he looked soaking wet. He was shivering and trying with no success to light a cigarette with a lighter that didn't seem to work. In silent disbelief I whispered to myself, *John?* I said it so quietly that I knew there was no way he could have heard me, but then eerily, as if he had, he looked up at me. Was I dreaming? It couldn't be him.

As far as I knew, he was still in the hospital. Besides, with his injuries there was no way he'd even be able to get around himself.

With everyone else in the house still asleep, I ran from my bedroom and down the stairs as fast and as quietly as I could, being careful not to wake anyone and scare him away. I threw open the back door. I thought it strange that this person should have the same build and gait as John as I watched him walk down the lane. I decided to follow. I watched him from behind as he continued to make his way across Old River Road and down into the marina, never bothering once to yield to the traffic that seemed to not even notice him, as it raced past from either direction.

When I got down to the marina, it was very dark; I noticed there were no stars or moon to light the sky, only stifling summer air infused with the stench of the rapidly approaching low tide. I ran down the dock behind him yelling, "John? Wait!" My heart pounding and my bruised, swollen eye throbbing with pain each time my feet hit the ground, I tried to catch up to him. Never turning around, he ignored me as he walked straight to the end of the dock, and then he was gone. But where? There was no sign of him. When I got to the end—where he seemed to vanish into thin air—I sat down on the dock holding my hand over my injured eye, trying to make sense of what I had just seen. Had he made some miraculous recovery and signed himself out of the hospital? But why were his clothes still wet? Was it that he'd been walking in the rain for hours? Was it even him that I saw? There was a faint bumping sound that seemed to come from the same side of the dock where he'd just vanished. I slowly and cautiously leaned over the edge and saw my boat—the same boat used in John's jump! It was untied and hitting against one of the pilings. How could it have possibly found its way back here?

I didn't know what to do: tie it up or let it go. I didn't want to touch it. If left alone, who knows how far it could drift downriver by itself... maybe Hoboken, Jersey City or beyond? Did the police already have the registration number? Too tired to think, I left the boat where it was but didn't secure it. With the tide going out, it wouldn't be going anywhere now anyway. I walked back to the house, took some aspirin, and climbed back into bed. Tired or not, heat or no heat, bed was where I planned to stay. It had been a long night. I tossed and turned for what seemed like hours. The sun was up when my mom came into my room with the news that John had died.

"When? What time?"

"Around 2 a.m., I think. Such a tragedy! His mom is all alone now."

***

We Catholics in town knew that if the weatherman predicted a stifling, hot day outside of church, you could bet on your life that the inside of the church would be twice as hot because keeping parishioners cool, comfortable and safe from heatstroke was practically equal to devil worship.

Or so it seemed, considering that had always been my experience for as many summers as I could remember, since I first set foot in this particular house of worship. Excepting the priests' individual comforts—one of which was having expensive steaks clandestinely delivered to the rear entrance of the rectory on Fridays during Lent when for the rest of us, it was fish or nothing—comfort and Catholicism were two concepts that, when it came to its parishioners, simply did not exist. And regarding the hot weather, since the Son of God had endured nails and thorns for hours on the cross, we, the churchgoers should not only have been able to sweat bullets, but I supposed the clergy thought making us sweat was also good practice for what it might be like to weather the fiery depths of hell, because according to those same priests, that's where most of us likely would end up since none of us had been blessed with their innate infallibility. And so it was a cruel joke that the giant, useless floor fans—like the priests themselves delivering their sermons—only ever blew hot air.

This was the last place I wanted to be on a Saturday morning: stuck inside a Catholic Church and sweating bullets. I didn't know if it was all the repetitive hand motions and chest-beating, the constant sitting, standing and kneeling, or the altar boy flinging incredible amounts of incense smoke in my face that was getting to me, but I was beginning to feel extremely nauseous.

Since today was John's funeral, I had to be here. It took him three days to die. The *Metropolitan Times* confirmed that the force from him hitting the water had pushed his legs, along with some of his organs, up into his body. I was surprised that it was such a tiny article tucked away in the middle of the paper. It read that he was found on the beach, under the bridge, and that the police were led to his location by an anonymous caller. The piece questioned whether it was murder or—as all outsiders often surmised about our town—alcoholism due to depression, which ultimately brought on suicide.

Since John's death, neither Dunn, Hale nor myself had been questioned by the police about our possible involvement, and I hoped things would stay that way. After Dunn and Hale acted like they cared so much about John, and then showed how tough they were by sucker punching me, neither one of the cowards had bothered to show up at his funeral. Carl chose to even though he had opted out of watching John's jump. He was forced to stand in the back, along with Jane and Steven, since most of the town was there and all the seats were taken. My brother informed me that it was a good thing that there were no seats left because the Captain, his imaginary friend, had to be somewhere else anyway and couldn't make it. I tried to imagine what pressing engagement a sea captain that's been dead for a hundred years could possibly have. Out of curiosity, I was about to ask Will where it was that his friend had to be, but the priest demanded everyone's attention.

Mrs. Kelly had been in denial all along about the fact that her son was dead, and there was also a problem with the circumstances surrounding his death, as there always is with bridge jumps. Was it attempted suicide or attempted murder? Since John couldn't speak for himself, and no one else had the courage to come forward, including myself, the police couldn't be sure, mostly because of the fact that when John was found unconscious there was a fair amount of alcohol and drugs in his system. When it came to bridge jumps, foul play or murder always had to be ruled out first, even though most of the time it was suicide with no one else involved except the victim, but because of procedure, it had to be determined if any of the marks on his body could have been there before his fall. I had read that he'd fallen more than 200 feet, and most likely went about eighty miles an hour to zero in a matter of seconds. What probably saved him at first and prolonged his life for a few days was that when he hit the water, he did so feet first and at a slight angle. But what also had to be determined was if the midsection of his body, which had been found so severely bruised and purplish-black in color, was injury entirely due to the fall or had some of it been inflicted first by someone else? Most likely, the experts concluded that the bruises were a result of the massive internal hemorrhaging he had suffered from multiple blunt force injuries when he made contact. It was a miracle that he didn't die right away. And yet, all of us cowards knew how he'd sustained those horrific injuries and still chose to leave him there all alone, not even knowing whether he would survive or not.

Most of the town was at the funeral, including old, eccentric Aunt Maeve. She loved attending any town functions, including funerals, because since the town was so small, she knew almost everyone, and she also knew that meant she'd usually be invited back to whichever grieving family's house to indulge in as much free liquor as she wanted afterwards, courtesy of the family of the deceased. Aunt Maeve was everybody's aunt. None of us ever knew if she was actually related to anybody. She had moved from Manhattan years ago and had felt like many New Yorkers: that coming to Pleasant Valley was like being on vacation in the country. Where she lived in the city, she had never been able to see fireflies or bluebirds, hear mourning doves or crickets, or have the chance to smell newly mown grass or wild roses. Even the rain smelled better in Pleasant Valley, she'd say.

Everyone knew she liked to drink, but then half the town did too, so who cared? She fit right in. All the kids in town loved her. In appearance, she was a large, pleasant woman with a ruddy complexion who wore flowery print dresses that were always popping buttons when she laughed. I think it was mostly out of loneliness that she was so generous. She had always hoped to marry and have children, but things never worked out. So she welcomed all the town's children as her own, and none of us had to wait until Halloween to ring her doorbell. As far as she was concerned, you were never imposing.

Other times of the year she always had something to offer, too, like cookies, cake, or lemonade. She'd give the kids chalk to play hopscotch in front of her house, while she sat on her porch and watched.

She'd even play board games, pick-up-sticks and jacks with her own version of lemonade close by, and despite the alcohol, her deftness and perception were no match for her opponents since she very rarely lost a game.

I noticed that the only available place left in church for Will and I was next to her, and that wasn't a good thing since besides the flowery print dresses, she'd always wear to formal occasions those fox stoles that had the vicious looking animal heads with feet attached. Will wouldn't sit next to her for that reason, which meant that I had to sit between Will and Aunt Maeve since he was afraid they'd come to life and attack. And Fritz, our dog, disliked them, too, probably even more than he disliked the poor seagulls, who knew when he was at the marina that there'd be no resting allowed for them on the dock pilings. Whenever he was forced to be around the birds, or Aunt Maeve's dead dog wrap, he would never show any fear; he was always ready to fight them at any moment should either decide to provoke him.

Because of his droning, I began to imagine the priest as a large male bee. I remembered how this very same priest frightened me as a child and was the reason I'd stopped going to church. He seemed to be a permanent fixture, since he'd been in the parish for decades. As he stood there before us saying Mass, he was much older than I had remembered... ancient and decrepit. He had to be pushing a hundred, at least. Even in his youth, he had always been tiny and frail, with a face that was skull-like and a severe underbite that accentuated his rotten, protruding teeth. It had been drummed into my head week after week, not only by him but also by the nuns who taught catechism that "God only came to the Catholics." This was something that when I'd repeated, my Protestant father and relatives of his same faith understandably didn't appreciate very much.

I remember this same priest in his younger days referring to us parishioners as "creatures of your ilk" whenever we'd line up for ashes, palms or to receive. He'd even shout at us in an accusatory tone not only from the altar but also from inside the confessional, a place where the confidential, private secrets were supposed to be shared in whispers and exclusively between the parishioner and the man God supposedly spoke through, which according to this old priest was not surprisingly none other than himself.

As a child being raised Catholic, weekly confession was mandatory, which meant that sometimes I'd have to make things up by the end of each week just so that I'd have something to confess. Trying to commit sins on a weekly basis just to have something to divulge was a mentally exhausting job for me, as I'm sure it was for most of the Catholic boys and girls who were like myself, as they prepared themselves for the sacraments of Holy Communion or Confirmation and were only between the ages of six and ten years old at the time! Every Friday, I dreaded stepping into that creepy, dark, vertical, double-sided coffin-like box known as the confessional, while I waited in silence for the skull with the rotten, protruding teeth to slide open his little trap-door, revealing nothing more than his silhouette, the sound of his breathing, and a wire screen between us, while the only signal for me to begin was him clearing his throat through the darkness. I was always to start with, "Bless me Father, for I have sinned" even though most times—like my other six-to-ten-year-old, so-called partners in crime—I hadn't. It became more and more difficult as the weeks went on for me to admit to one of the two major sins the Catholic Church recognizes mortal and venial sin, but I would never have dreamed of saying, "Bless me Father, I haven't sinned" because it wasn't allowed. So, as the weeks went by and my friends and I would discuss what we might possibly fabricate for each passing week, we became quite good at making things up, or to be honest, lying, because we weren't allowed to leave the confessional until we came up with something, anything, no matter how trivial. I remember one particular week when I had gone reluctantly into that dark box, knowing there were those behind me waiting their turn in the pews, so I quickly tried to think of something to confess. I decided to pretend I had missed Mass the week before, even though I hadn't. I had completely forgotten that this was considered a mortal sin: "a grave matter committed with intention." Missing Mass was equal to murder in the eyes of the church. Being proud of myself that I'd come up with something to confess, I admitted to missing the Sunday that had just passed. Through the darkness, the priest's hushed, calm tone suddenly gave way to screaming. I'm sure his anger was heard by the entire congregation outside the confessional, after which I was given a very long penance to be said immediately at the altar.

From that day on, I began to question the church's rituals, and saw them as silly and man-made.

For instance, why was it OK at one time for a Catholic, no matter how grave the sin that had been committed, to buy his or her way into heaven with an indulgence? Could other religions pay their way out of hell, too? I took it to mean that Catholics were allowed to commit as many heinous crimes as they wanted, so long as they were rich. Also, why did I have to go to confession every week if I didn't actually commit a sin? And did Limbo and Purgatory really exist? What was the difference between the two? Why did the pope need a summer home? Wasn't the Vatican big enough? Why did God supposedly only come to Catholics? Why were the priests the only ones allowed to eat meat on Fridays during Lent? And, most importantly, since I was taught by nuns and priests that God is everywhere, and a church can be wherever there are two or more persons, why then did I have to go sit in some building at the same time every week or else be considered equal to that of a murderer? I knew none of my questions would ever be answered, so that day I literally thanked God out loud that the confessional was situated right by the exit. I had decided to skip my lengthy penance since walking to the altar would mean having to walk past everyone who had overheard my traumatic experience. I also decided right then and there to never step inside a Catholic Church again, but John's funeral was different. I had no choice.

It was collection time: time for the long-handled baskets to be shoved in front of our faces. Even at a funeral, the Catholic Church had to make money. It wasn't enough that the organist and priest had already been paid for the service, not to mention the yearly tithes received from so many of its members. Will hadn't noticed that the basket had reached us, since he was preoccupied with his gaudy, hand-painted tie depicting a hunter shooting at geese that my grandfather had bought for him from a souvenir shop in Canada; it was the only tie he'd ever wear. I, on the other hand, was preoccupied with my pockets, which to my surprise were empty. Since I'd missed countless Sundays, I hadn't planned on taking communion anyway, so it looked like I wouldn't be giving or receiving.

The casket sat on its bier in front of the altar with Mrs. Kelly seated directly behind it. I looked over and saw the mournful look of despair on her face. I watched her as she wept silently, while she stared up at one of the many stained-glass windows, as if she expected John's spirit to come flying through it at any minute.

She and John had a very different look at Mr. Kelly's funeral a year ago. It was almost one of relief—and they both had good reason to be relieved. I remembered countless nights between midnight and dawn when the screaming would go on for hours. Through the darkness, Will and I would peek between spaces in our bedroom blinds, while the shadowy figure of Mr. Kelly would yell relentless obscenities at the house that chose to lock him and the darkness out; the house that—year after year— sat in silence and never once replied to his drunken rants. And yet, some would dare call the police. How could they when Mr. Kelly was once a policeman himself? The next morning, it was as if nothing had happened, Mrs. Kelly going about her gardening and greeting neighbors as they passed by the yard. No one ever knew that Mr. Kelly, being locked out, had been forced to spend the night sleeping on the pool table in the garage. In a way, I missed those days. Mrs. Kelly was right, with John gone, too, it would be much too quiet now.

***

My mom had offered food and drink to anyone who wanted to come back to the marina after the service, since not only was Mrs. Kelly all alone now but also overcome with grief and not up to the task of entertaining. I was never good in these types of situations: emotional ones. I never knew what to say. I was even more uncomfortable knowing that Mrs. Kelly—because of the marina's location—would be forced to look in the direction of the bridge all day; the very thing that had been such a source of sorrow for her. Much of the day my mom had spent sitting with her. I heard them reminiscing about when John and I were small and how fast the time went. How John would never swim near the bridge when he was little, even though all the other kids did, because his father had told him about the many men who had built the bridge that had fallen to their deaths, or died by getting sucked under the mud and concrete, and how that would always make the bridge a sort of tomb.

"Funny," she said, "how I'm hearing all this talk around town that he jumped and that no one pushed him."

At least she was able to muster a smile while she watched Aunt Maeve indulging in beer and whiskey. But she wasn't the only one indulging in free alcohol all afternoon. We all realized when we saw him acting strangely that Fritz had slyly been helping himself to the beer that had accumulated in the washtub under the tap. He no longer seemed threatened by Aunt Maeve's fox stole. He forgot about it for the moment and had decided it was time to devote his full attention to terrorizing seagulls.

As far as he was concerned, none of them were allowed to rest for even a minute on the wood pilings, and he kept himself busy by barking at them and chasing them.

Everyone, including Mrs. Kelly, had noticed my eye. Ike had guessed it was "girl trouble." I let it go at that—if it would save me from having to volunteer what had really happened.

"How've you been, Will?" Mrs. Kelly asked my brother.

"I'm fine. The Captain said to tell you he's sorry."

"Who's the Captain?" Mrs. Kelly said, the question meant for Will, but instead she looked at me to answer.

"Oh, he's my brother's friend," I volunteered with a wink.

"Will, you'll have to point him out to me. Is he here?"

"Not yet, but he will be."

I could see that Will had Mrs. Kelly convinced that the Captain was of this earth, an actual living, breathing person. When he was out of earshot, I didn't even bother to explain. Lately the lines between the dead and the living seemed blurred. The dead seemed to be part of my everyday world: Ike's stories about ghosts, Will's Captain, and now John. I wanted to tell her that John came to me at a time when I wasn't sure if I was awake or dreaming and that I dreaded his visits. That I felt I was losing my mind from lack of sleep and losing sleep from fear of dreaming. But was I dreaming?

I wanted to tell her that Will and I were sorry that we were both responsible in a way for her son's death, even though the boat was stolen. And how so many of us had watched him jump. And even though I was the one who'd thought to call police, we'd all left him there to die alone anyway.

I noticed Steven, Jane and Carl sitting on a bench in front of the boathouse with their drinks. I excused myself from Mrs. Kelly, took my drink, and decided to go out and sit by them. As they watched me walk toward them, I thought to myself that this might be the perfect time to let them know I'd seen John the night he died, then walk them out to the slip at the end of the pier and show them that the boat came back... all by itself. But I just couldn't. Not now, anyway. I wished Ike hadn't told me that I was careless by not securing it, and then tied it up himself; it would have been long gone by now, out of my life.

As soon as I sat down next to them, Carl said, "We were just

wondering...what if *the man* comes around here asking questions?"

"I don't know, but it's making me pretty paranoid. Whether
the police think it's suicide or murder, what proof do I have that I
wasn't in on it?" I was pissed off, not at Carl but at being dragged
into a situation I wanted no part of, so I downed my drink quickly
and went and got another. As I walked by Aunt Maeve, I noticed
she was either dozing or passed out. I also noticed Fritz, as he ran
past me down the dock with her long-dead, fur wrap in his mouth.
Too far from him to save it, I watched him stop and carefully let it
drop from his mouth over the edge of the dock into the river.

Steven, Jane and Carl saw him too, and looked at me, as they
laughed in surprise. I put my finger to my lips. It would be our
secret when Aunt Maeve woke.

She Walks Like a Bearded Rainbow

When I was six years old, I remember the sugar factory in the south end of town, which had been there long before I was born, had mysteriously caught fire in the middle of the night. It made the air smell so incredibly sweet that no one considered, for even a moment, the hazardous predicament the poor firemen had to endure as they fought the tall flames, while standing knee-deep in melted sugar that was thicker than Hollywood quicksand and as hot as molten lava.

At the time, people said it was probably "Jewish lightning." I had heard that expression mentioned once or twice before in my short life and began to wonder to myself if that meant that Jewish people were able to make lightning appear at will. And if so, could they also control other act of nature? Fascinated, I remember thinking at the time that why couldn't I have been raised Jewish instead of Catholic. There seemed to be nothing extraordinary or exciting about being Catholic; all I'd learned from my experience was that it was frightening, tedious and uninspiring.

What was left of the deserted factory was a skeleton of a building with empty elevator shafts, a lot of shattered windows, and as I've said before rats as big as cats. Like most industries in town, it sat on the river's edge, and there was a dirt road leading to it that we'd drive in on, although it was a good idea to first turn our headlights off, so no one could see us entering...especially the cops.

Because of its location, it helped to have a car. It was one of the few places we could go to drink, since in 1968, the legal age was twenty-one in New Jersey. If we drove over the state line to New York—which a lot of us often did—it was eighteen there.

That meant that both driving and drinking skills had to be mastered simultaneously, making anyone who was eighteen a novice at the extremely difficult task of being able to hold the wheel and hold their liquor at the same time.

The abandoned factory was the place where everyone gravitated toward, the place where one could participate in—and I'm being sarcastic when I say this—certain ingenious or should I say, unsophisticated, small town diversions like shooting BB guns at the giant rats and other cerebral pastimes like popping wheelies or witnessing some new kid's "initiation." Still, other forms of entertainment included indulging in cheap wine, or smoking someone's idea of "good homegrown," which was almost always bad. I'd usually just show up for the wine and weed since I wasn't really into shooting vermin, or beating the shit out of someone just for the hell of it. Luckily, having to witness initiations didn't happen too often. And being a public school kid, I'd been very lucky to have managed to escape one myself.

The factory was also the last place I remembered seeing John alive before he went through with his ridiculous bet. It was pretty late, but since neither of us could sleep, Jane and I decided to go there. The reason we both couldn't sleep was partly due to our constant worrying about the draft, but mostly why John had to pull such a stupid stunt. I reminded myself daily that he was the first person to die that was my age, and a person who was at one time in my life a very close friend.

We drove in slowly. Jane remembered to turn the lights off, as the dirt and gravel crunched loudly beneath her car's tires. Two police cars passed each other on the main road in opposite directions, but neither one bothered to see us. We parked, shut the engine and rolled down the windows. All we could hear were the crickets and the low hum of the city that faced us across the river. We were the only ones there at that late hour. Jane asked if we could stay in the car since it was so dark that she was afraid we wouldn't be able to see any of the giant rats if they decided to wander by our feet. The river in front of us was like a piece of black glass, as it reflected an upside-down mirror image of the bridge perfectly lined up against itself in the distance. I proudly pulled a fat joint—the stuff that always made me think too much—out of my pocket. Jane cautiously looked around, as if expecting to see someone in the darkness. When she didn't, she reached into the glove compartment of the old German car and pulled out a silver hip flask that she had filled with Seagram's. Then with some difficulty, but refusing help, she cranked back the sun-roof by hand.

There were a lot of stars, which was unusual considering the constant light pollution from the city and the amusement park that bombarded us from either side. She pressed the lighter in and we waited a long time for it to pop out. She retrieved the glowing metal gadget, then pressed it against the joint.

The red glow from its tip was the only visible thing that would give us away, as we tried to hide out there in the dark.

"At least this is one thing I can count on in this car to work."

"And a very important thing, too!" I added, but after a few hits, the pot had my mind wandering again and I found myself thinking this town had way too much darkness and way too much light and at all the wrong times.

She laughed at my lighter comment, but I could see she was sad, pensive, somewhere else. We each took turns taking a hit. She put her head on my shoulder, which made me tense up since I'd always been secretly attracted to her. She'd never known my secret, but then she'd never gotten so physically close before. I couldn't help but wonder if she behaved like this when she was alone with Carl. I tried to put it out of my mind for the moment.

"Is everything OK?" I asked, trying to distract myself from my own thoughts.

"Yeah, I'm just thinking about everything, mostly John… how we shouldn't have left him lying there. I wake up every night thinking about it, and I can't go back to sleep."

"You and me, both! I regret not trying to talk him out of it. But with those injuries he never could have survived. He was just too messed up."

"When you think about it, everybody's messed up these days," she answered. "Everybody and everything. It seems like the whole world is messed up lately. I can't believe...first, Martin Luther King is shot dead then Robert Kennedy. It's been a crazy year, so far! And those soldiers, our own soldiers, supposedly killing all those innocent women and children. And the riots here at home. Why do you think that there's always so much hatred and death in the world?"

I didn't answer. We both just sat there in silence staring at the bridge, as we shared what was left of the joint. Then she looked up through the sun-roof and pointed overhead. Breaking the silence, she said, "That's a planet."

"Which one?"

"See that big one directly overhead? Mars, is it? I forget, but I know it's not a star."

"How can you tell?" I ask.

"Because only stars twinkle, not planets, and that one's not twinkling."

"Is that so?"

"It's a whole other world up there, isn't it? This sad, sorry excuse for one down here might as well not even exist with all its assassinations and riots, because in relation to the rest of the universe, wouldn't you agree we're pretty insignificant?"

"Insignificant...yeah...kind of like those of us on this side of the river. On that side, the bridge leads to the city that never sleeps. This side, New Jersey... might as well be oblivion."

"Well, just because you can't see us on the horizon doesn't mean we aren't there, or here, or however that saying goes." She laughed.

We sat there quietly for a long time, and the tide started to change. She stayed resting on my shoulder. Her hair smelled so clean that I wanted to touch it but held back. "Let me have some of that whiskey," I asked, so that maybe I could force myself to stop thinking about touching her. She raised herself to a sitting position and passed me the flask. I took a swig that burned like hell going down. She grabbed my thigh and squeezed it. Her action left me wondering if I should risk our longtime friendship and make a move until she blurted out, "Hey, are you up for a murderburger?"

Disappointed, yet relieved, I said, "Sure...I could never say no to one of those, or twenty, or thirty!" We split for the nearest White Castle, hoping to find it still open.

***

July had dragged on, but eventually we found ourselves in the "dog days" of summer, as the older folks in town liked to refer to August, and every year they would. I used to wonder where that expression came from until I found out that it had little to do with actual dogs, and more to do with astronomy. Supposedly, way back when, the Romans noticed that Sirius, the Dog Star—which is also the brightest star in the sky—rose and set with the sun at that same time of year, August. They believed this star helped to increase the warmth of the sun, making the sky even hotter.

As if the incredible heat wasn't bad enough, after seventeen years of being asleep the locusts had come back. The last time they were around was before Will was born, and I was so young that I barely remembered the destruction they caused. The ground was covered with them. They hung from trees and even found their way into our mailboxes. The scene reminded me of the plague of insects that the Bible predicted would happen right before the apocalypse. I was glad they didn't return when I was learning about the plagues in catechism, otherwise I'm sure I would have thought it was the end of the world right there and then. Although, along with the carnage of the Vietnam War and current events, the end of the world wouldn't have been so hard to imagine.

For Steven, Jane and I, graduation and everything that had to do with it was a distant memory. The summer had been crawling by, but we really didn't mind since none of us had given the slightest thought as to what we had planned to do regarding our futures...none of us guys, anyway. Jane was the only one actually saving money to go away to college. It was already too late for the fall semester, but she was hoping to begin in the spring at a well-known art school in Philadelphia. To raise money toward her tuition, she had just recently begun working for Lenny as a bartender at the Lookout.

Since it was Lenny's day off, Steven, Carl and I decided to pay her a surprise visit. She'd probably be there all alone, without any customers because it was still early in the afternoon. The Lookout didn't draw much of a lunch crowd, so to speak, unless of course, it happened to be in liquid form.

We expected to open the tavern door and see her usual smiling face. Instead we found her sobbing. She stood behind the bar with the phone in her hand, tears running down her cheeks. When she looked up and saw us, she immediately hung up the phone. The three of us couldn't imagine what tragedy had transpired. It was clear that she looked extremely relieved to see us.

"What's wrong? Were you trying to reach Lenny?" I asked.

"No, I was trying to call you, Henry. There's a gigantic rat in the women's bathroom. It looks dead, but I'm afraid to go near it. It's floating in one of the toilets. Lenny always tells me to make sure I close the doors behind me if I'm bringing out the garbage or having deliveries brought in. I always do. There's no way it could have gotten in anywhere."

I told her that it most likely got in through the plumbing system. I also let her know that rats are incredible swimmers, so they're good at staying underwater for long periods of time. They've been known to swim through miles of pipes.

"Well, if they're such great swimmers, why did this one drown?" she asked, while trying not to laugh through her tears.

The three of us then went into the women's bathroom to assess the situation, while she waited outside. Rats were always a big problem in Pleasant Valley since the town sat right on the waterfront.

I once heard that rodents love water more than garbage, but even so, the town had a trash collection every night so that the garbage never had a chance to sit for too long and ferment, giving the rats more of a reason to hang around.

"You're right! That thing's big! Not Japanese-science-fiction-movie-big, but at least the size of a small dog! Do you have something we can put it in like an empty beer box, along with maybe a large garbage bag?" Carl asked, not too enthusiastically. "Also, do you have something we can use to get it out of the toilet?"

"I think Lenny keeps a small shovel outside in the back for putting down rock salt," Jane offered, while making it clear that she wasn't planning on moving herself from behind the bar until the dead animal was gone from the building.

It was definitely dead, and heavy and black, with a tail so thick that it almost looked like a lion tamer's whip. We triple-wrapped it in plastic garbage bags and threw it in the can behind the Lookout, making sure to put a heavy rock on top to prevent raccoons from being able to open it—not that anything could prevent those animals from opening a trash can lid.

When things settled down, Jane poured us some drinks on the house out of gratitude. "I'm so glad you guys decided to stop by. If I had called Lenny, he would have said to just take care of it, deal with it and not be such a baby. He would have never come down here on his day off. I was so worried about how I was going to get it out of there before customers started coming in. It would have been the first and last time for a lot of them, if they saw that!"

"That's what we're here for!" Carl said, as he winked at her. He studied all the bottles on display behind the bar and then asked "Hey bartender, how can you remember the recipes for all the different drinks people order?"

"I'm learning as I go along. Lenny helps a lot. Besides, the Lookout isn't a fancy place, it's more like just an old man's bar. I rarely get anyone asking for stuff like martinis, gimlets or sidecars. We don't even have a wine list! It's mostly just beer and shots these guys want. Screwdrivers and seven-and-sevens are probably the most exotic drinks I've been asked to make, so far."

"Hey, do Dunn and Hale ever come in here anymore?" I asked, feeling weird sitting at the bar since the last time we'd done that John and his friends were sitting here, too.

"Not that I know of. Not on my shift anyway. As far as I know, I don't think anyone has seen those guys around town. At least, I haven't seen them since you got punched in the eye." She reached out and gently and sympathetically used her fingertips to examine that area of my face.

Maybe I was imagining it, but Carl quickly attempted to divert any attention I might be getting from Jane by interrupting, "Hey, do you think John had all his money with him when he jumped? You know, what he was going to give Dunn and Hale if he lost the bet? If so, someone probably found a hell of a lot of bills floating in the river the next day."

"Or...since they knew he was unconscious, maybe it was still in his pocket somehow, and Dunn and Hale took it from him when they pulled him out of the boat, and left him on the beach," I said. "It was so dark, who would have been able to see them do it?"

"You should join the Pleasant Valley Police, maybe become a detective." Jane joked.

The attention was still on me. This time, Carl got up quickly to play something on the jukebox. I was enjoying this. Suddenly I knew how it felt to be treated like him by the opposite sex, for a change, and he clearly couldn't deal with not being the center of attention—for once in his life—when it came to women. He made his feelings obvious when he put on a Blue Cheer song that was so loud Jane and I had to practically shout over the music.

"I'm trying to stay as far away from the police as I possibly can!" I yelled over the song.

"Anyway, what are you guys up to today?" Jane yelled back.

"Not much," Steven said. "Would you happen to know where we could get some weed? A dime or even a nickel? Everyone we've tried so far today has been dry."

Jane's expression suddenly changed. "So is that the real reason you came to see me? Can't you guys get through one day without getting high? The three of you need some serious goals. Get out from under this town. There's a whole world out there."

"I don't see you making any plans for the future," Steven snapped back.

"What are you talking about? At least I'm saving to get out of here! What exactly is it that holds you guys here? Nobody ever seems to want to leave this place!"

The song had ended, and Carl decided to come back and sit at the bar, adding, "Why should we when we've got everything right here, including pretty bartenders."

Jane just rolled her eyes, "You guys are hopeless."

"So, I guess I'm getting this sermon, too?" Carl continued to provoke. "You do realize that I'm a lot older than these guys?"

"Exactly," Jane shot back. I think it was the first time I'd seen Carl blush, plus he had that same child-who'd-just-been-scolded-by-his-mother look again.

The liquid-lunchers began to arrive. Steven, Carl and I put our money on the bar and got up to leave, but Jane wouldn't take it. "Later...and thanks again; you guys saved my life."

"No problem." Carl mumbled, still blushing.

She intentionally looked down, wiping the bar with a towel. I guessed it was to avoid having to make eye contact with any of us. For some reason she seemed annoyed, especially with Carl. At that point, I noticed that all the attention was back on him, as usual, even though it seemed negative. I had to wonder then, what kind was better. Was it because, as I suspected, she secretly had a thing for him?

Season of the Witch

The air was chilly and filled with that unmistakable scent of burning leaves. Even though October meant the boating season was coming to an end, Carl was still needed at the marina. I was already at the Castle attempting to collect him, but as usual he took his time drinking coffee—not that there was any reason to rush.

From the Castle's lack of heat, he kept an old, tattered blanket wrapped around him as he sat at the kitchen table with me. He was about to light a bowl and share it when we heard someone knocking loudly on the front door. What was strange about that was that no one usually knocked on Carl's front door. He never bothered to lock it because he'd told almost everyone he knew in town that he was OK with his friends just walking in. He'd always believed privacy was a state of mind; that is until this stranger happened to invade that same right to seclusion he'd always regarded as absurd.

Eyes wide, Carl look frightened as he slowly rose from the table, motioning for me to keep silent. He carefully crept to an area by the front door and quietly positioned himself with his back to the wall at the side of a window, so that the man or woman couldn't see him. From Carl's vantage point, he saw that the unwelcome guest was a man.

The stranger called out in a very cordial voice, "Hello? Is there anybody home? I'll just take a few minutes of your time." As if the man could see through walls and knew Carl was there hiding, the trespasser waited a long time but never once would he be so rude as to rattle the doorknob to check for himself if the door was unlocked. Later, Carl would say he thought that was pretty courteous and admirable of the man, considering Carl was the real trespasser in this situation and also considering how intimidating the man looked. What scared Carl most about him was that he wore a tie, carried a briefcase, and he had that military regulation crew cut, which made him look very official. I knew Carl didn't want anything official in his life; he was done with that. He'd chosen to leave the establishment world and all it represented far behind.

When Carl saw that the visitor had finally walked away, he slowly and carefully opened his front door and was surprised to find an eviction notice tacked to it. He had been given sixty days to vacate the premises, no questions asked, considering he was there illegally. The land had been bought by a Mr. Sterling Hilliard—the man who had recently begun buying up most of the waterfront in town— and Carl guessed maybe the same man in the suit and tie that had just been at his door.

Carl came back and sat down with me, pulling his tattered blanket tightly around himself. He proceeded to light his pipe and let me know that the Castle would soon be history.

"What are you talking about?"

"Some nice corporate douche bag just tacked an eviction notice to my door. I have two months to get out. The Castle's being torn down to make way for...a fucking apartment complex!"

"What?" I sat there with my mouth open in disbelief. Soon it would be Halloween, then Thanksgiving and Christmas; there couldn't be a worse time to be evicted. It was bad enough that Carl didn't have any family to lean on, which was his own choice, but to be evicted around the holidays just seemed cruel.

With that said, he insisted we finish the bowl. He'd need a lot more tokes than usual to get through this day. Carl then put his head in his hands and said, "It's bad enough that I'll be losing my pad, but why does it always have to be something historical that gets torn down or blown up?" It bothered him that such a celebrated, authentic area would be razed, forced to give in and relent, like himself, to what those money-hungry assholes called "progress." He figured that also meant that his neighbor at the bottom of the hill—the one with the electricity—also was being forced out.

***

Soon after Carl got his notice, a construction site sign went up with a rendering of what the enormously hideous apartment complex would look like. Sadly, at around the same time the sign went up, the stone gargoyles that had been keeping a vigilant watch over Carl's kingdom began to disappear one by one, getting stolen until there was only one left.

Like Jane, Carl was a procrastinator and never worried today about what he could put off until tomorrow. So even though he was aware of the eviction notice attached to his front door, after that day he never bothered to pay much attention to the date that was written on it. He went about his business and chose to plan his annual Halloween party as if there was no eviction notice. Either way, every year his friends—myself included—looked forward to it. Locals from town and friends from across the river, including some very well-known artists and musicians, would show up bearing gifts of LSD and liquor, music and marijuana, peace pills and patchouli, and even pumpkins. It was always a privilege to be a guest at one of his parties.

***

I had been hoping for an Indian summer, but so far October had just been filled with a cool, silent impenetrable fog, days when the sky, the bridge and the river water all blended together into one dismal color—gray.

I sat at the end of the dock staring off in the direction of the bridge. It was somehow easier to look at in the daylight. Except for the sound of a distant foghorn and the sad cries of seagulls overhead, there was an uncomfortable stillness in the air. I decided to visit Mrs. Kelly, not only because I still felt guilty in some ways for John's death but because things were slow at the marina.

Carl was with some new conquest, and I couldn't find Jane or Steven anywhere, so I didn't know what to do with myself. My mom was hounding me for weeks to stop by and ask her if she might need help with anything, since she was all alone now. No one ever saw her leaving the house anymore, and she wouldn't even bother to answer the phone, or the door when my mom attempted to visit.

John had never been much help around the house. Anyone who happened to pass by their yard could tell by looking at it that nothing had really been done in the way of repairs since Mr. Kelly's death.

The paint was peeling, some of the shutters were broken, and it seemed with each passing fall new leaves had obviously added themselves to the old forgotten piles.

Since Mrs. Kelly didn't answer the front door, I went around to the backyard where everything was overgrown, and I found myself almost up to my waist in weeds. I cupped my hands over my eyes as I leaned into the screen door's frame. Although the yellowed shades on all the windows had been drawn, making the inside of the house very dark, I was able to see Mrs. Kelly as she sat at the kitchen table staring into space. She was talking to someone, but from what I could see, no one was there. I guessed then that she must have been talking to herself. The phone began to ring, but she took no notice of it; she just went on talking as if there were someone out of view and seated just across the table from her. Hanging on the wall next to her, she still had her photo of John Kennedy next to a calendar that was, from what I could see, crossed out only up until the day of John's death. Every day since that day was left unmarked; it was as if she were living in suspended animation, frozen in time. The phone had finally stopped ringing. I thought this would be as good a time as any to gather the courage I'd need to announce my presence. I tapped lightly on the well-weathered doorframe, not meaning to startle her, but I obviously had.

"I'm sorry, Henry! I didn't see you standing there!" she said in her thick Irish accent, while she held her hand to her chest, as if to slow her quickened heartbeat.

"Come in, please—it's so good to see you!"

"I came to see if you needed help with anything," I answered, barely able to look at her.

"Yes, actually. Come in and we'll talk. Excuse the mess. I

haven't felt like—or had much practice at—being social lately. Would you like some tea?"

Still managing to avoid eye contact, I found myself saying yes.

"Good. We'll have it in the dining room. Come in and have a seat. I'll be right there. We'll talk, and then I'll show you what needs to be done."

From where I was seated in the dining room, I could see Mrs. Kelly fidgeting around for spoons, cups, and tea bags in the kitchen. As I sat waiting for the kettle to boil, I took notice of my surroundings. Besides "Irish lace"—my mom's name for cobwebs—that seemed to hang from almost every corner of the room, houseplants in dire need of water, dishes piled up in the sink, and the long-neglected mail, there was wood paneling that had been painted with semi-gloss, acoustic ceiling tiles that held up an out-of-place chandelier, a modest collection of Belleek in the china closet that was lit from within, beveled-glass frames that held black and white photos of the Kelly family's ancestors from the old country, and—last but not least—the same fiberglass drapes I'd hidden inside and twisted myself up in when John and I once played hide-and-seek. That would be the first and last time I'd ever use drapes as a hiding place, especially ones made of fiberglass, since I was left feeling like I had thousands of tiny glass splinters embedded underneath my skin for days.

Mrs. Kelly came into the dining room and set down our cups, along with a tin of cookies, apologizing that they were most likely stale, then she sat across from me. The whole time we were in the dining room she kept her chair turned sideways away from the table, as if she wasn't capable of being fully relaxed anymore.

"It's very quiet here now, Henry. It's so quiet, it hurts my ears! I just can't for the life of me understand why John would have done such a foolish thing."

Wanting to say something, I looked at her. Now would have been the perfect time to tell her that I knew he wasn't pushed because I was there and saw the whole thing. The words were in my mind, but I just couldn't say them. I only hoped he hadn't intentionally tried to take his life.

She let out a sad, pathetic sigh. The whole time she spoke, she looked at the floor. "I always wished for quiet when Mr. Kelly was alive. You know what they say about wishing for things."

Because of her intimidating beauty, it was difficult to make eye contact while I offered up my mediocre painting, carpentry and landscaping skills. She looked up at me, and before I could look away our eyes locked.

"Well, I'd certainly appreciate any help I could get. I have some of Mr. Kelly's old tools in the basement, if you'd care to take a look."

She stood at the top, as she watched me go down the basement steps. It was another musty nineteenth century basement just like most houses in town, its floor made from the same bluestone cliffs that had for so long now been blamed for sucking the light out of our Pleasant Valley. The bare bulb with a pull chain had blown out long ago, she said, but since it was daytime I was able to see, even though it took my eyes a few seconds to adjust.

I felt strange opening Mr. Kelly's toolbox and thought for some odd reason that it might provoke his spirit, and I might then end up hearing his voice from some dark corner of the basement asking me what I was doing in his house looking through his toolbox. Watching from the steps, Mrs. Kelly pointed to a shelf above my head by an old wooden workbench. I carefully took the box down and opened it, feeling the whole time that there might be more than one set of eyes watching me from behind. There were screwdrivers, a rusty, loose-handled hammer, a couple of brads and screws, some picture wire, and a putty knife; that was the extent of it. A real Irishman's toolbox, I thought, minus the duct tape. And as far as being able to help with cutting the grass, the mower was manual and didn't even have a motor, just blades that rolled around when it was pushed.

As I began making my way back up the steps, Mrs. Kelly started to come down to the basement but stopped halfway. She stood blocking the stairway, so I wasn't able to get past, and asked if I'd found everything I needed. I avoided her eyes again and said

I'd found everything. What wasn't here, I'd bring from home. I started to ascend the steps to where she was standing right above me. She didn't move out of the way. Face-to-face, she leaned into me, whispering into my ear a question that I never expected to be asked: "Henry, have you seen him?"

"Excuse me?" I answered, knowing as soon as the words came out of her mouth what she had probably meant.

Just then, on what had seemed a perfectly clear and cloudless day so far, a flash of lightning and a crack of thunder seemed to come out of nowhere.

"I really should go now, but I'll be back." I saw the sudden change in weather as an opportunity to escape without having to answer her question. "I really should go," I said, avoiding her gaze. She didn't respond but stayed where she was, arms folded across her chest, as she watched me climb the steps and leave the house. By the look on my face, she knew... I didn't have to tell her.

***

With Halloween came Carl's long-anticipated party, a welcome respite not only from the tragic events that had an effect on all of us—not to mention, assassinations and the war—but from our own tragic event: John's death, which really seemed to have no effect on the outside world at all, just our little world—unfortunately, mine in particular.

The coming of Halloween also signaled Steven's last few days as a civilian. He had sprung the shocking news on us that he'd been drafted. Even though we pleaded with him not to go and Jane offered to drive him to Canada, he refused. He also refused to take us up on our offer to try and help him get out of going by pumping him with various, multiple drugs on the day he was to report. Drugs scared Steven. He had always been such a straight arrow; he would rarely even drink. He also felt there was no point in trying to dodge the draft because whatever scheme he might come up with, they'd be wise to him. Jane told me that she cried for days when she found out. He made a promise to her that he'd write as often as possible, and he'd get his tour of duty over as soon as he could so that he could get back home in one piece—unlike a lot of others who were his age. And so we all felt like we needed Carl's party to unwind since, like the changing season, we felt like everything else around us was changing, too, little by little, except maybe not for the better this time. Saddled with as much beer and wine as we each could carry, the three of us hopped the wall in darkness to climb the stone staircase to Carl's lair. The night was cold and clear. The warm glow of the Castle was surrounded by black silhouettes of towering, majestic trees. Sharply defined against the Castle's inner glow, their delicate tracery reminded me of a much larger version of an ornate *scherenschnitte* lamp that my mom had when I was younger.

We could hear evidence of the electricity Carl had borrowed from his neighbor who lived at the bottom of the hill as the sounds of Moby Grape, as well as the smells of pot and patchouli, drifted down past us. I remember reading that people from India first used patchouli to mask the odor of sweat. I began to wonder which one was worse!

When we got to the top there was strobe light spilling out from the old stone house, the pulsating flash matching the beat of the music and making everyone's movements in the yard look sequenced. I overheard someone who passed by me ask someone else, as they referred to the strobe effect, if that was from the acid they had dropped earlier or if the light was really doing that?

The three of us then attempted to work our way through the crowded yard. Some of Carl's friends who we didn't know were sitting on the grass, listening intently to a man playing an acoustic guitar while he sang. We headed for the candlelit kitchen, where some obviously stoned guests were discussing the meaning of the monolith in the recent movie that had been out for a few months called 2001, and if we'd really be capable of such a thing as time travel in the future. A few others in the kitchen who weren't involved in the monolith conversation had just discovered what they believed to be the amazing concept of putting peanut butter between two Ritz crackers, which they couldn't seem to make or eat fast enough. Carl was in the middle of admitting to his guests that both the monolith and the Ritz crackers had been enough to "blow his mind," when he suddenly noticed us entering, grabbed Steven by the shoulders, and announced, "This fine young man you see before you is off to fight in the war! Help me try and persuade him not to go before it's too late!" Carl's friends—all strangers to us—laughed briefly and then went back to whatever they were talking about, as if Carl had said nothing and the three of us were invisible, all except for one girl who offered an empathetic, "Oh, no!"

Hearing this, Steven smiled to himself, happy to have gotten such a sympathetic response. By the looks of her, she might have been a little older than him and very pretty, too. She moved closer to Steven adding, "You know, my friend knows a soldier over there who said we recently killed a lot of civilians, including women and children—on purpose—but our government is keeping it a secret. At least Johnson halted the bombing for now, so things might get better if you get sent there. I can't believe we've dropped 800 tons of bombs for three and a half years! For what?" Steven told her he agreed, but he felt he had no way out, he'd have to face it. Maybe with any luck, he wouldn't get sent there.

Carl came over by us then with a tray of peanut butter crackers and directing the lyrics at Steven, sang, "'Mister, You're A Better Man than I'... it's not really like any of us has a choice, though, right? Unfortunately, we can't all run off to Canada." Then he said, "Try this!" but quickly changed his mind and took the tray back. "Wait! First try this." He handed us the bong instead.

Eventually, everyone got around to asking Carl about the note on his front door, what he planned to do and where he would go. I offered him to stay at the marina for as long as he wanted.

Hell, half the girls in town who were already holding onto articles of his clothing also had offered him a place to stay, Jane included. But as if the notice was nothing more than an annoyance, his only answer had been that he had intended to take the thing off the door before the party, he'd just forgotten.

He decided he'd rather not talk about it that. He didn't want to talk about anything that would bring him down, not then, not ever.

Out of the corner of my eye I noticed but couldn't comprehend why there was a girl sitting on the kitchen floor across from me, blowing hash smoke into the drain hole of an empty Igloo cooler. She seemed to be doing it for no other reason than solely for her own entertainment. I wouldn't find out until much later that the subject of her experiment was a live animal. Carl's cat was inside. Would he be OK with that? Did he even know?

At some point, my legs began to feel like rubber. With a warm beer in my hand, I made my way for the living room, where I was happy to become one with a still paisley, once velvet, empty sofa I found. As the night wore on, the more I had to drink and smoke, the deeper I sank into the cushions. I began to imagine gravity as two large invisible hands holding me down. I couldn't have gotten up if my life depended on it. But my life did depend on getting myself up off the couch, since before I'd left the kitchen, Carl had put me in charge of sitting close to the stereo to not only adjust the needle on albums—should any of them start to skip—but also flip them over when each side finished playing.

Thankfully, I still had the endless *In a Gadda Da Vida* to get through, which someone had just put on the turntable, meaning it would be a while before I'd have to get up again and begin putting on the large pile of vinyls that were stacked in order of what was to be played. *Disraeli Gears* then *Axis* were up next. The assignment Carl gave me didn't seem so bad, since Steven and the anti-war girl joined me on the couch and both took turns getting my drinks so I wouldn't lose my most important seat.

Next thing I knew, I was waking to early gray light as it softly crept through the windows. Night was gone, and I was lying alone on the couch shivering. The silent house made me wonder if Carl's generous neighbor—the one with the electricity— had not "gotten lucky" by conquering one of Carl's "hippy women" during the night, since both he and the extension cords appeared to be gone. Or had I slept through, missing him leaving with both?

Steven and the anti-war girl were passed out on floor, wrapped around each other, with Jane close by. There were also a lot of others scattered about sleeping. The carved pumpkins that had been donated for the party seemed to have completely different expressions than they did the night before.

They looked weary and exhausted. I'm sure I was imagining things, but that was the first time in my life I'd remembered pumpkins' carved faces looking the way I felt, hung over.

After I relieved myself outside, I stumbled into the kitchen where I found Carl making coffee. He handed me a cup while he got one for himself and then motioned for me to get the sugar. I joined him at the table.

"Bummer about John," he said. "You know, even though I always thought that the guy was an asshole, I still think about what a tragic waste his death was. Plus the fact that those clowns had to go and rip off your boat!"

"But them using my boat isn't the worst part." After I said that, I realized maybe I should have kept my thoughts to myself.

He bent his head down so that he could see me better over the top of his McGuinn-like shades. "Go on, I'm listening," he said, as he nimbly balanced an album cover on his lap, while dipping his fingers into a Baggie to roll a joint. At that moment, an attractive girl in an almost transparent robe passed by, stroked his hair, took his cup of coffee for herself, and then left the room. He kept on rolling the joint and didn't even seem to notice that his coffee cup came and went.

"Was that the infamous owner of the purple pants?" I asked.

"What purple pants?" he answered, as he twisted and licked rolling papers together, lighting the joint then inhaled and passed it to me. I had to wonder to myself if the reason he could never seem to remember any of his relationships with the opposite sex was an effect of too many drugs or too many women...or both.

"Do you believe in ghosts?" I found myself saying, knowing I'd most likely regret my question.

"The night John died, I saw him in my yard then I followed him to the marina, where he disappeared."

Then, like Carl just woke up from a dream himself, he said, while straining to hold in his breath and talk at the same time, "Where's my cup?"

"Trying to change the subject?" I said laughing, as I passed back the joint. "Am I going crazy?"

"No. I do believe in ghosts, especially when they have unfinished business. Maybe he's trying to tell you something." Then he answered with a halfway decent impersonation of Bela Lugosi, "Could it be, John's got some kind of message for you from beyond the grave?"

"I don't want any message. I wish he'd just leave me alone! The weird thing is that I think his mom's been seeing him, too. Not only that, but...the boat seems to have come back all by itself."

"Your boat? When? How? No wonder you're freaked out!"

"There's a possibility that the tide could have brought my boat to shore. The bridge isn't that far from the marina, but coming back to its exact slip is a weird coincidence, don't you think?"

"You mean your little boat being able to float itself right up to the dock? Hell, yeah! And how do you know that John's mom has been seeing him? Have you been in contact with her since the funeral? I heard she's like some kind of shut-in now."

"I went over to her house to see if she needed anything."

"Oh yeah? Like what? Just what exactly were you thinking she might need?" Carl smiled while raising his eyebrows.

"Damn! Nothing like that! You know...like repair jobs, cutting the grass, whatever. Have you even seen the place? What a mess, both inside and out. While I was over there, she asked me if I'd seen John, almost like she knew I had. I didn't answer her. I haven't told anyone but you. I haven't even told Steven and Jane. I feel like I'm going crazy. I'm afraid to sleep. At least I got some sleep on your couch last night. I felt safe for the first time in weeks knowing most likely that he wouldn't appear here, and even if he did and was sitting right next to me, I probably wouldn't have noticed him anyway with all these people around. I'm not afraid of him. I just wish he didn't look so real, so... solid. I always thought ghosts were supposed to be, you know, see-through, right?"

"Did you ask Will if his captain friend is see-through?" Carl joked, still doing his Bela impersonation.

I just shook my head while I gave him a look.

Then Carl said in a seemingly serious and mature tone, "Sorry, man. Hey, you're welcome to stay here as long as you want, that is, until they kick me out!" Then Carl looked directly over my head and said, "You too, John!"

"Very funny, Carl. Fuck you!" I said. I laughed but at the same time shuddered. That's the one thing I hated about weed. The stuff always made me think too much, especially that early in the morning, making me wonder if there were such things as ghosts or life after death and if they really existed.

The girl in the transparent robe came back and took Carl by the hand, leading him out of the room. He looked over his shoulder as he was being pulled away from the kitchen, though obviously not against his will. He winked at me. "Later, man," was all he said.

Suddenly I was all alone and realized there was a strange, muffled sound coming from the far end of the room. With everyone still asleep and Carl gone, I could only hope the sound I was hearing wasn't John deciding to pay me a visit now that I was finally by myself. I forced myself to get out of my chair and investigate. I found the poor cat who, for some reason was still trapped in the cooler.

I released him from his prison, then went to find my shoes without waking Steven and Jane. I'd be seeing them at the cemetery later today anyway. I hopped the wall outside. A lone gargoyle—the only one remaining that hadn't been stolen yet—quietly watched me go.

***

From Carl's to the marina was a twenty minute walk, all downhill. I expected to find Ike on the dock already washing his face in the filthy river. Still early when I got there, I noticed that no one was awake yet, not even him. The boating season had gone by so quickly. I stood looking at all the boats still in the water that had to come out, the same ones I'd felt like I'd just helped put in, yet they were already being dry-docked again.

Today was the first day of November, or All Saint's Day, a day I was taught by the Catholic Church that they'd much rather have children of their faith celebrate than Halloween, but where was the fun in that? The weather was very warm and brought a fleeting glimpse of the Indian summer I wished we had. Out on the Hudson, a hot white mist hung in the air making the tall city buildings look like soft, undefined shadows of themselves.

I regretted having given myself such a bad hangover from the night before, but at least I looked in slightly better shape than I'd remembered those pumpkins, which wasn't saying much. I decided to lie down on the dock with Carl's borrowed radio for a little while to rest my eyes. He wouldn't have minded. The sun felt good on my face, while the radio by my head blasted out what was new with Vietnam, Vanilla Fudge and the Velvet Underground. A lethargic freighter silently struggled upriver against the faint, fuzzy silhouette of a skyline. The last remains of summer's sweltering mist had seemed to swallow up all definition of shape and sound except for the radio waves. I must have dozed for a brief time because John had crept into my dreams again, and I was starting to resent it. He came up the ladder from the dock and began to talk to Will but ignored me. Then I overheard John ask Will to go with him for a boat ride. At that point, I had to ask myself if he was real, since even though somehow I knew I was dreaming, I also knew that John was dead. I tried to stop them, but Will ignored me and followed John down the steps, as they climbed into our little aluminum boat. Will waved as they rowed away, John with his back to me, guiding the oars through the water, but I noticed that neither one spoke to the other. I watched myself run to the end of the dock, screaming for Will to come back. He didn't seem to hear but just kept smiling at me, as John rowed away from the dock.

Just then, I felt someone kicking the sole of my shoe. The sound of Carl's radio slowly came back as I woke from the dream, and I could hear the Amboy Duke's "Journey to the Center of Your Mind" playing. I looked up, shielding my eyes from the sun, and standing above me was Ike.

"Where's Will?" I asked, panicked.

"He's in the boathouse talking to his invisible friend about pirates and who knows what else.

Listen, an inboard has been towed here and is sitting out on the lift. The bottom has been ripped out, probably another victim of the same sunken barge that your dad's boat hit. Such a shame that had to happen now, at the very end of the season."

This was going to be a long day considering that after my work was done at the marina, I still had to go to the cemetery, where so much vandalism always resulted as of Halloween. And as much as I tried to distance myself from John's spirit, or whatever I'd been seeing, I'd given Mrs. Kelly my word that I would look after John's grave, since he was buried there, too.

***

Once a month, Steven, Jane and I were on the cleanup committee for the local cemetery. It was volunteer work, but I didn't care. The graveyard had always been one of my most favorite places. The 300-year old cemetery had headstones that were both elaborate and simple. And for such an ancient, peaceful place, there couldn't have been a more unconsciously appropriate reverberation than the bells from the Riverside church across the Hudson, as they'd echo daily off the Palisades behind us.

I expected things to be much worse, since this place had always been considered one of the most popular Halloween hangouts in Pleasant Valley. I was relieved to find, at least, that only some of the older, historic stones were knocked over and smashed. That the older ones had been broken never really came as a surprise because every year that was usually the case. The rest of the mess was just empty or broken beer bottles. I was glad to see that John's grave was left untouched. Aside from reporting the damaged stones to the Historical Society, we were also in charge of removing weeds and poison ivy, replacing some unbroken stones that had been toppled by the vandals, and raking up dead leaves, ones that always seemed to find their way to the north side, or "devil's side" of the cemetery. The gravedigger there had told us once that—like most old graveyards—when this one was founded, the north side was reserved for suicides, murder victims, and the unbaptized, since the living believed that these were the unfortunate souls who would never be allowed into

Heaven. Then there were the unknowns, those who had drowned while on sinking ships only to wash ashore at King's Ferry, their nameless graves marked only by small, blank white stones.

The Seventeenth Century cemetery might have been the only one in the nation that had a railroad built underneath it. The trains no longer ran, but the tunnel was still there. Usually on Halloween, after the local kids would sit among the gravestones, drinking beer and getting high, they'd go down into the tunnel and scare each other with stories of zombies and Indian ghosts. Once again, the dead who were buried above would have their peaceful sleep interrupted just like decades before when the noisy and inconsiderate industrial machines rode beneath them. The tunnel was filled with discarded beer bottles, cigarette butts, and unearthly shafts of light that shone through in the daytime. In some places, if you looked up, you could actually see the rotting wood from the undersides of some of the caskets poking through the dirt. At night, you didn't go in unless you had a very dependable flashlight. I'd heard that for some reason matches never seemed to stay lit.

Some minor celebrities were buried in the cemetery, their graves bordered by extravagant iron fences, separating themselves from those considered less significant in life: the ordinary infants, children, sailors, and the wives who wore out widow's walks waiting for their husbands to return. The wives, judging from the dates of death on their gravestones, seemed to outlive their spouses by decades, and I'm sure if given the choice would have chosen not to die so long after their mates. Besides Dutch settlers and sea captains, there was also the friend of Buffalo Bill, an Indian princess, some soldiers from the Civil and Spanish-American wars, and the man whose ferry served as a vital instrument for arranging meetings between George Washington and his senior officer the night before the Battle of Fort Washington.

I'd usually bring Will and Fritz. Will would help to rake leaves, taking a rest every once in a while to sit on any bench that had an accompanying grave. Having a comfortable place to sit was common back in the days when relatives would come and visit the graves of deceased family members.

Will loved moving from bench to bench, talking to the dead. Fritz would follow him as if my brother were a medium from some séance, while he talked to the Indian princess, the friend of Buffalo Bill, the soldiers, and sea captains, and the man who ferried George Washington across the Hudson. The way Fritz tilted his head to one side, as he'd watch Will and then look at the ground, you'd swear they were getting answers from below.

Jane and I followed Steven's lead as he let go of his rake, deciding to take a rest. He leaned against the cemetery wall and slid all the way down until he was sitting on the ground. The cemetery had already seen centuries of carefully chosen symbolism set in stone, everyone a desperate attempt by grieving mortals that to this day were still trying to comprehend the mystery that is death. As I wiped the grimy sweat from my face with the front of my shirt, I took a look around at all the different headstones and thought of what their symbols meant...that is, according to Rusty. He was the lonely and chatty old gravedigger who had shared with us, on more than one occasion, the meanings of those symbols carved in stone whenever he'd happen to be working on the same day as us, taking a break with a drink from whatever he kept in a brown paper bag, the contents always a secret.

Surprisingly, for a cemetery, there weren't many angels, but there were a lot of doves, the messengers of God, which we had been told stood for peace. Also, the cemetery had a few horses.

Rusty told us that the likeness of a horse carved in stone symbolized goodness, unless the horse was black. This cemetery had no black horses. Besides the anchors that obviously denoted sailors' graves, but which could also signify hope or eternal life, there were the not so obvious ones like draperies, which would represent mourning, or the urn which was a token for the soul, or a broken branch which stood for an untimely death. Pine cones signified a full, long life with children, while instruments like harps and lyres, if their strings were broken, meant a break in mortal life. An upside down torch designated the end of life. And finally, while a small, empty chair specifically meant the death of a child, the Victorian symbol of a child asleep stood for death itself and not necessarily that of a child.

The old gravedigger's name was Russell Winterburn, but he'd rather be called Rusty. Hunched over and always in need of a shave, he said that the older he got, the better the name fit since that described what his bones felt like, having to dig graves by hand with a shovel because the ground was too weak from the tunnel beneath to be able to support the weight of a backhoe.

"Be careful where you sit, there's poison ivy everywhere." I motioned to the wall behind Steven.

"This place might run out of room soon," Steven said, wiping his forehead on his sleeve. "All the graves seem to be taken."

"I'm pretty sure the graves are recycled every hundred years and then can be sold and reopened.

I guess that means whoever goes in next goes on top," Jane said, as she laughed.

"If they keep piling bodies on top of each other, what if they start falling through...into the tunnel?" Steven added.

"Hey, do you want to go down there and have a look around?" Jane was obviously a lot braver than any of us.

"Not really—what if Fritz ends up finding some weird kind of bone, and he wants me to play catch with him?" I answered.

"Remember when Rusty told us that in Victorian times people used to come to cemeteries for picnics, wanting to spend the day with their dead relatives?" Jane offered, as we noticed Will sitting on one across from us, on the other side of the cemetery. "He also said that back then wreaths of flowers were placed on graves to create 'magic circles' that were believed to confuse the dead person's ghost to prevent the corpse from leaving the coffin. And that the reason coins were put on someone's eyes when they died was to prevent them from opening, since it was believed that the first person they'd be able to look at after death would die next."

I thought then of John—being the most recent person to be buried at the cemetery. Jane looked over at me, noticing that I had suddenly become quiet. She said I looked deep in thought and asked if anything was wrong. I said nothing. Even though I was fighting the urge, I wasn't about to tell her or Steven what I had told Carl earlier...at least not yet.

"You wanna know something, Jane? You're goddamn morbid, and so is Will!" Steven said, nodding in my brother's direction. "He's been conversing with the granite since we got here."

As he said that and we glanced over to where Will had been sitting, we realized he was gone. Since none of us had seen him and Fritz leave through the front gate, all of us agreed that the only place he could be was the tunnel—the one place I had always tried to avoid.

"Can you guys help me find him?" I pleaded. The three of us left our rakes and quickly began walking to the back of the cemetery where there was a small, downward slope of a hill. Embedded in the hill and partially covered by thick, tangled, overgrown ivy, was a large, ornate, and very rusty iron gate, which was the old train tunnel opening. Even in daylight, we needed a flashlight if we wanted to see beyond the gate into the tunnel. I thought I could hear Fritz barking.

"Great!" I said. "He better not come out of there with anything other than Will!" Now I was able to see movement since some sunlight was shining through in places from above. Will came running to the opposite side of the gate with Fritz, grabbed onto the iron bars and stuck his face through.

"What do you think you're doing? You can't just wander off like that! Come out here now!"

"I was looking for trains," Will answered.

"There's no trains here. Not anymore."

"But...I just heard one. Wait! Be quiet! Do you hear that?"

We all stood on the outside of the gate, looking in at him. I could see that Fritz was full of mud, and I shivered to think about where he might have just been exploring. "Will, there's no trains; there haven't been for years. Come out now! Don't make me come in there!"

"Like you would!" Jane said, laughing at my threat.

He ignored me and stood quietly with his eyes tightly closed while listening intently, hands still gripping the bars. At that moment, from somewhere behind Will, I could swear that an underground wind, like some passing phantom train, blew air under the crypts and through the tunnel opening in our direction, air that was stale and silent...dead air. Will then took his time letting himself and Fritz out of the gate, calmly closing it behind him.

"Hurry up! Wait till mom sees Fritz, he's filthy!" I said, as we all walked away from the tunnel, Will being the only one who looked back.

Castles Made of Sand

J ohn was the only one I had to blame for my going four months without a decent night's sleep. I used to be afraid of when he might appear, but I'd only grown annoyed at the sight of him. I had to admit, though, that if given the choice, confronting him in daylight was much easier than when I'd wake to find him quietly standing in the dark at the foot of my bed, which seemed to be his favorite place to visit. His look was what always got to me, that vacant stare.

I watched as everyone went on with their lives, free of John. I thought about Mrs. Kelly. What did she mean when she'd asked if I'd seen him? How could she have known he was appearing to me? I guessed that maybe she'd been seeing him, too. Carl was the only one I had told, but I wasn't sure if he'd taken me seriously. I wanted to tell someone other than him, since I felt like the whole thing was driving me to a need for psychiatric help. Steven had already begun his tour of duty, and Jane was in Philadelphia at her new school getting set up for the spring semester. More than my parents or grandfather, Ike would be the only one who would believe me. But I didn't want Ike or them to know that I was there the night John jumped, or that my boat was the one John and his friends had used.

One morning I found myself ambling around the docks and boathouse, trying to keep busy, as usual, trying to pretend that I didn't see John, so much easier to do in the daytime, out in the open.

As I glanced up, I saw someone hobbling down the hill toward the marina. He was followed by a cat and appeared weighed down by a pack on his back, barely able to hold all the stuff he was carrying.

As he got closer, I noticed the man was Carl. He looked completely exhausted and out of breath, as he threw down the duffel bag, along with all the stuff he'd been carrying. The cat stopped with him, then sat by his feet watching me, as if waiting for Carl to tell his story.

"What's up?"

"I'm out, man! The Castle is being torn down as we speak. They almost took me down, too. You should have been there! I was in the middle of having this crazy dream, in 'Nam running through these jungles, tripping on these giant vines. Above me, there were these helicopters everywhere. I remember getting shot, and this soldier I'd never seen before was cleaning the blood off my face and pushing down on this gaping hole in my chest. The pain was so real! And this guy had no fear. He kept chanting over and over again how I should try and get home, that the war was nothing but a bad trip. Then I woke to reality and total devastation, man. Giant machines were coming through the walls, and this fucking cat was sitting on my chest the whole time licking my face! I guess I should have paid more attention to that note on my door."

"Damn! What did you do when you realized what was really happening?"

"I was relieved to find out I wasn't really drafted but not so relieved when I found that the sound from the helicopters in my dream was really from bulldozers and that everything around me was being razed!" Carl held the same philosophy as Jane: You should never worry about today what you could worry about tomorrow. In a lot of ways, they were both procrastinators, but he was even more so than her. As summer faded into fall and winter was approaching, he had actually forgotten all about the eviction notice, and now he was left with no choice but to run as he quickly grabbed whatever he could carry: clothes, albums, books, his stash, the cat. He hadn't planned on taking the cat; he just wanted to get the animal out of danger, away from the chaos.

"The bulldozer operators watched me as I ran," Carl continued. "I had to get out of there in a hurry. Those guys with their massive machines made themselves clear that they weren't going to wait. Without stopping for even a second, they went right on with their destruction. I thought about how strange I must have looked to them and to others that drove past me as I was trying to escape, while holding onto all my stuff with the cat racing close behind. I felt like some scared, helpless rabbit running for his life. I looked back only once to see the walls of that historic place being crushed like a cardboard box, along with my stereo and what little furniture I had."

"I'm so sorry to hear that." I pointed to the stuff on the ground. "So this is all you have left?"

"This is all I could carry. Here...I want you to have these. I know you'll take good care of them."

He shoved a pile of his most treasured albums at me.

Shocked and saddened that we'd lost one of our hangouts, not to mention Carl's historic home, to so-called progress, I said, "You can stay with us for as long as you want. You know my parents would be OK with that." But after my suggestion, I wondered how long my parents would really be able to put up with the late-night comings and goings of his frequent romantic flings and drug deals.

"Thanks, but the time has come, I think, for me to split this scene. I just wanted to stop by and thank you guys for everything. The Castle being torn down is just one more sign for me that the whole vibe is changing."

Regarding the "vibe," I usually had no idea what the hell he was talking about since he was always using that *hippie/freak* lingo, but this time I understood completely because I had been feeling like everything was changing, too. And not just in Pleasant Valley but worldwide. Listening to him was like listening to someone speaking English, but every so often he'd insert a foreign word here and there that I'd have to try to quickly translate in my head just so that I'd be able to process the rest of his sentence. Sadly, now that Carl was moving away, I was finally starting to understand him. I asked, "Where do you think you'll end up?"

"I thought I might try hitching a ride on Route 80 since that road goes clear across the country. I was thinking California. I know some cats from L.A. who live in a canyon not too far from

Hollywood and Sunset. They'd be willing to let me crash at their pad for a while until I got my shit together."

"Were these 'cats' with the 'pad' ever at any of your parties?"

"Yeah, remember those dudes from San Francisco? They said Haight used to be the happening place, but the scene there has become more like the fuzz vs. the freaks, plus the freaks quickly tired of putting on an unintentional show for all those tour buses. So, Hollywood is where it's at now."

Tour buses, show, for what, I thought but didn't bother to ask. I probably wouldn't have understood the explanation anyway.

With winter fast approaching and only ten days until Christmas, Carl was now homeless.

That had to be the worst time of year to be homeless and hitching, especially in the Northeast.

"What are you going to do about your boat? You can't hitch with a boat, and even if you wanted to put the boat back in the river, you couldn't. There's way too much ice."

"I should have put the thing up for sale a while ago."

"I can pay you what you want, or I can keep the boat here for you. I wish you'd let me do that. I'd like to hope that someday you might be back this way."

He didn't answer. Then he said, "I also need to find this cat a home. I never planned on taking him with me, but I couldn't leave him there with nowhere to hide." Up to that point, the cat had been walking circles around Carl, getting as close to him as possible, and then rubbing itself against his legs. Suddenly, as if the animal heard Carl, he walked a few yards away from us and climbed into his boat, curled up, and went to sleep. Carl looked at me, and we both laughed.

"We'll have to see what Fritz thinks about this, a cat living at the marina," I offered.

"Is Will here?"

I led Carl into the boathouse where Ike and Will had been busy cleaning out storage lockers, while my grandfather sat watching them. When Carl told them he was leaving town for good, even though a little early for Communion, my grandfather got out the shot glasses anyway. When Will requested one for his friend but not himself, my grandfather poured one for the Captain, too. I wasn't surprised at Will's request, but I have to admit, I was actually relieved to see the glass remain on the bar, full of whiskey and untouched. A real apparition or not, I knew the Captain probably would never show himself to me, but I wondered if John could resist now, especially with the temptation of an unclaimed drink sitting there. He'd never been able to resist one when he was alive. And I knew, too, that I'd forever have that image in my mind of him smoking a cigarette in my backyard on the night he died, only to find out later that he'd never left the hospital, had never even regained consciousness.

Anyway, I wasn't going to bring that up. Carl was the only one who knew, so I have to admit, I was a little startled to see Carl at that exact moment lift his glass as he turned to face that direction of the bar like he was about to toast someone who wasn't there. He downed his shot quickly. "To the Captain!" he said. Carl winked at me, and it was only then that I realized he'd just been appeasing Will.

"To the Captain!" we all repeated, while looking in the same direction at nothing. After a few heavenly rounds of spirits, my grandfather shook Carl's hand and patted him on the back. "We'll certainly miss you, and you know you're always welcome here. Where are you headed?"

"Los Angeles, probably Hollywood."

"Ah, the land of fruits and nuts!"

"Yeah, they definitely live a much healthier lifestyle out there, I hear."

I realized then, as clever and well-read as Carl was, that my grandfather's joke had gone right over his head.

My brother started to cry. Carl attempted to make him feel better with the promise of sending him something from Hollywood and told him to come visit with me and to stay as long as we'd like.

Then I walked with Carl to Jane and Steven's house so he could say goodbye. We knew Steven wouldn't be there. He had been in accelerated Basic Training for the past six weeks. Then he'd be shipped off to the nightmare that was Vietnam. It was a definite. None of us could even begin to imagine the atrocities of war that he had yet to witness.

When Carl told Jane he was leaving for good, she threw her arms around his neck. "Do I have to let go?" she asked. Her hug seemed to make him very tense, almost like he didn't know how to react.

He looked as if he was restraining himself. Instead of his customary, casual loverboy stance, he became robotic. He kept his hands on her arms, gripping them like he wanted to pull her away from him as quickly as possible. I was curious as to why he was acting like this since I knew that he knew I had always secretly wondered if something had gone on between the two of them, something more than friendship. I'm sure he knew I'd never be brave enough to come right out and ask, and he knew he'd never be the one to tell. I was beginning to think he found a certain pleasure in always making me wonder. That's what made his reaction to her hug seem all the more stranger to me.

"When I told you guys to get your act together and get out of this town, I was hoping that would be after I had left for Philadelphia since I've never been good at saying goodbye," Jane said.

"Hey, I'm still here!" I chimed in.

Carl laughed and saw that as a chance to break from her grip. He quickly pulled out a joint from his coat pocket. "One for the road?" he offered. We passed it around a few times, then he said that he should get going while there was still daylight.

"Don't be a stranger, come back and see us," Jane pleaded.

"Yeah, give us a call, or send us a postcard from Hollywood," I joked, but I was feeling just as sad as Jane.

Carl winked. "I'll see you in the movies!" And he was off with his duffel bag and weed, looking like his Henley and bandanna were tailor-made for him, up on Old River Road with his thumb out.

These Days

I heard the familiar, daily sound of our metal mailbox clanking closed and my mom wishing the mailman a Merry Christmas, as she stepped outside to get the mail. Going by the weather, Christmas Eve would be rainy and dismal with no actual snow, only sleet and slush in the forecast.

I missed Carl, yet at the same time I envied him. He had the courage, just like Steven and Jane, just like those seagulls I'd always watch fly away, to finally leave this place and get out from under its shadow.

Lost in thought, I sat at the kitchen table, reading the back of a cereal box to Will when mom came back into the house. As she stamped her wet feet on the hall mat, she yelled that there was a package for us. She set the parcel wrapped in brown paper on the kitchen table. I immediately knew by the return address that the box was from Carl. Even though most of the lettering was smeared from the rain, the word California was still legible. Giving into curiosity, I quickly tore open the box and found a letter alongside a wrapped gift for Will. I made no mention of the letter, and even when mom had asked if Carl had written. When she was at the kitchen sink, not facing me, I pocketed the note. Although Will was disappointed, I persuaded him to put Carl's gift under the tree to be opened after dinner with the other presents.

As Will was summoned to the living room to help mom get ready for our dinner company to arrive, I ripped open Carl's letter as fast as I could and began reading its contents in secret, debating whether or not I should share it with anyone at dinner, especially Jane. Since she was driving home from Philadelphia for the holidays and spending Christmas Eve with us, this would be the first time Carl would be far away, and I'd have her all to myself.

I began to read that Carl's cross-country trip had been a "real downer." Not long after he'd left town hitching, a big rig driver picked him up and offered him a ride, at least halfway, but stole all his stuff and left him stranded at an Iowa truck stop during a blizzard. The only thing the guy didn't steal was his weed. A waitress at the truck stop restaurant was kind enough to offer Carl her apartment for the night.

I thought how he'd always been extremely lucky at getting women to bed in the past and even after being robbed and left in the middle of nowhere during a snowstorm, he'd still made time for yet another conquest. So I was surprised when I read further that he thought she was too old for him. She'd allowed him to spend the night at her place, and then the next morning he was lucky enough to meet two girls with a van at the local general store. They drove him as far as San Francisco, mostly because their dog had instantly befriended him in the parking lot. He then took a bus to L.A., where he spent the night with some homeless.

He wrote that he thought he might be in love. Carl never said stuff like that, even when I'd try countless times in roundabout ways to get him to admit he had serious thoughts about Jane or any woman. He never showed his feelings when it came to the opposite sex, so it was weird to hear him express those words of emotion so freely.

He wrote that he'd met a girl named Marina when he was trying to find the way to his friend's house in Laurel Canyon. He'd been walking a long time but wasn't sure if he was headed in the right direction. He saw her sitting in her car at a light and approached her. She gave him a ride, since she was going that way, too. Coincidentally, she and Carl had a lot of the same friends...

Just then I heard my dad calling to help with the tree. I pocketed the letter again and joined the family near our unadorned, ten-foot-high Douglas fir in the living room. For some reason, my parents kept a hectic tradition of putting up the tree on Christmas Eve, never before, which usually stayed up until January 6th, since my mom said that day was known as "Little Christmas." As Will and I helped dad with our annual chore of untangling the lights, mom got the boxes of ornaments down from the attic. A lot of them were old mercury glass ornaments from Germany that had been handed down through generations. Besides those, we'd put tinsel on the tree, but since Fritz loved so much to eat tinsel, we learned from experience to only hang it where he couldn't reach. One year, in an effort to get at it, he knocked the entire tree down, causing most of the lights to blow out and a lot of the heirloom ornaments to break. From then on, even though we made sure the tinsel was out of reach, we decided to tie the tree up with string and attach it to a nail on the wall.

After the tree lights were tested and strung, Will was always given the job of putting each ornament on, since this was something he looked forward to every year, and he was very precise as to each one's placement. My work was done, so I excused myself and began running upstairs to my room, where I could finish reading Carl's letter in private.

"So, was there a note from Carl?" my mom yelled to me when I was halfway up the steps.

"No, I didn't see one."

"That's odd. I hope he at least calls us to let us know how he's doing."

I didn't answer. Closing the door to my room, I took the letter out and continued reading. Carl wrote that Laurel Canyon was rustic, with winding roads and shady trees. The place reminded him a lot of Pleasant Valley, except there was no river. He'd spent his whole life living close to and looking at the Hudson every day. He went on to say that to suddenly not be around a large body of water anymore felt like a part of his soul had been taken away. But at least where he was, he wrote, was practically like endless summer most of the time.

He was working part time at a head shop on Hollywood Boulevard, a job that seemed perfectly suited to Carl, and he'd been invited to stay at Cass Elliot's house, who welcomed any and every music lover. I envied him when I read that he was meeting a lot of the "cats" on the albums he gave me. If he didn't run into artists like Jim Morrison, Frank Zappa or David Crosby at the local canyon store, he'd meet them at parties or clubs.

He closed by inviting me, saying I should bring Jane and Will. We would "dig the scene." He asked about Jane and wrote that he missed her and thought about her every day, and to tell her that she was "just as beautiful as the California girls he'd seen, and she should seriously come to Hollywood and become a movie star." With that, my decision was made. I folded the letter and placed it at the very bottom of my dresser drawer.

***

Besides the tradition of the tree being put up on Christmas Eve, it was also tradition that my mom would make my dad's favorite dish, sauerbraten, which she made the authentic German way by putting the beef in a large stone crock with peppercorns, vinegar, cloves, juniper berries, coriander, thyme, mace, ginger and mustard seed, and then letting it marinate in those spices for three to five days.

Will had been hoping we'd get snow for Christmas, as he did every year. Instead Pleasant Valley got cold rain and sleet, but nothing, I imagined, like the rain Steven would witness in Vietnam.

Our relatives from New York had been invited and were supposed to come for dinner, but they had to cancel at the last minute since a lot of the highways were flooding and icy. The George Washington Bridge was even closed because of high winds. So, besides myself, it was just going to be my parents, grandfather, Ike, Will, Jane and Aunt Maeve.

Jane was in Philadelphia. She had wanted to get settled into her new surroundings before the spring semester started so that the transition would be a little easier for her. But even with the inclement weather, I convinced her to come home for the holidays and spend them with us. I had extended the invitation to her not only so that she wouldn't have to be all alone and probably the only one on her campus, but so she'd actually have a place to go for Christmas and New Year's since her parents would be away. They would be spending the holidays in St. Maarten and had invited her to come along, but she declined. She said that she couldn't understand how they could go away on vacation and put Steven out of their minds while he was stuck in the hellish nightmare of Vietnam. Her mom's answer was that the trip would be a much needed distraction to temporarily stop her from constantly worrying about him.

Jane and Aunt Maeve had both arrived in time to watch us finish the tree. Aunt Maeve then began helping my mom with the last minute details of getting dinner ready. I noticed the fire was dying out, and since none of us had given any thought to stocking firewood close by, I decided I'd better walk down to the boatyard to get a few more cords before the fire died out completely. Jane offered to come with me to help carry the logs. I was glad that dad had covered them in plastic before the storm, or they would have been useless on such a rainy day.

As we both got closer to the woodpile on the side of the boathouse—slipping and sliding on the sleet-covered docks—I pointed to a young man standing farther out on the dock, watching us.

"Who is that?" I asked Jane. She was shivering while she held her coat over her head. At that point, the rain had started coming down in sheets, which probably made him harder to see.

"Where?" she answered, as her eyes followed to where I was pointing. I then realized she couldn't have been able to see anyone, since when I'd looked away for that second and then looked back, no one was standing out there.

"Never mind. I thought I saw someone standing at the end of the dock." I knew who I had seen, but I decided not to mention my dilemma, and we walked back to the house with the wood. Was there even one day that he could stay away and leave me alone?

As we dried off and got the fire going strong again, I had just poured Jane and myself some drinks when I noticed her reading the tags on the packages under the tree.

"Oh, Carl sent Will a gift? Did he write to say how he's doing?" Jane asked, unable to hide the disappointed look on her face, as if she'd wished Carl himself was under the tree instead. I pondered if I should show her the letter, tell her he'd invited her to come to

California and save the most important part for last, that he was in love, but I decided it would be better pretending there was no letter.

"Maybe. We'll see when Will opens his gift after dinner. I'm sure there's a note inside," I lied.

After dinner we all went into the living room where Mom had put out some traditional desserts. One was pfeffernusse, and the other was a German version of marzipan, two things I could definitely live without, but we all knew they were my mom's favorites. I disliked them both so much that to my surprise, I found myself reaching for that most dreaded dessert, fruitcake, courtesy of Aunt Maeve.

Years had gone by since my brother or I could wait until Christmas morning to open gifts, I could see Will eyeing the packages under the tree. I handed him Carl's to open first. The gift was a large glass bottle with a ship inside. As Will tried to figure out how the ship got inside the bottle, I pretended to look for a note in the empty box.

"There's nothing in here," I offered.

"That's strange. Let me see that." my mom said, refusing to believe Carl hadn't included a note. I crossed the room and handed her the box, knowing for sure it was empty.

There was that disappointed look on Jane's face again. Hoping to get her to stop thinking about Carl, I said, "Will, I see Fritz has opened his presents from Jane already, but why haven't you opened hers yet?"

Fritz had helped himself to his gift much earlier in the evening, since I'm sure he caught the scent of dog treats through the wrapping paper; at least it took his mind off trying to reach the tinsel.

Will hurried to open the gifts quickly. One was a drawing book, another a snow globe with a city scene of Philadelphia inside that he couldn't stop shaking.

"Looks like you finally got your snow for Christmas," Dad kidded.

Do You Believe in Magic?

J ane knew there was a good chance her campus would still be
empty for the holidays, so after Christmas, she decided that
rather than stay at her family's house in town or head back to
school, she'd drive down to the Wildwoods, a barrier island at the
bottom of New Jersey to spend New Year's Eve there. She'd invited
me to join her, and it didn't take much for her to convince me.
With her going to be away full time at school in January and both
Carl and Steven gone, my daily routine had gotten pretty boring,
not to mention downright depressing.

She told me that she only hoped her car would get to South
Jersey without giving her any trouble. I knew from driving with
her that she always carried a gallon jug of water everywhere just
in case the car overheated, which it often did, and she'd then have
to pull over to replace whatever water was lost.

We started out on the Turnpike, where getting onto the
shoulder to replace water would be a difficult stunt since this road
was somewhat like what I'd imagined the Autobahn, with
everyone going at their own speed. Even if you had your
directional on for miles, no one would be courteous enough to
ever let you pull over. I'd seen some pretty horrific crashes, too,
once what appeared to be an entire family on their way to or from
vacation. I remember broken glass, twisted metal, and their
mangled, bloody bodies, along with all their possessions strewn
all over the macadam, since even though everyone was usually
always impatient and ignored limit signs that were posted, there
were rarely any speed traps or police. The police often hid behind
the greenery of the Parkway, not the Turnpike. That was because
there was nothing green or growing on the Turnpike—nothing to
hide behind, unless you counted the massive stone and steel
structures of industry.

We passed the oil refinery in Elizabeth and then Newark airport, and even with all the windows rolled up, the chemical smell was still unbearable. I always thought how unfortunate that Newark, an international airport, was built in the middle of such industrial stench, since on being their first introduction to New Jersey, visitors not only from the United States, but the world, would forever question how the hell the word *garden* could have anything to do with the state.

When the time came to exit the dreaded Turnpike, we got onto the Garden State Parkway, trading the stench and speeding cars for shrubbery and state troopers, where we began counting the tiny mileage markers on the side of the road. We had 180 to go and wouldn't exit until the marker with the number four. Jane had gotten pretty skilled at throwing quarters into the exact change toll booths; she slowed down just enough to take aim as she tossed them into the metal receptacles.

I was surprised when she told me that half the hotels were open all winter and also about a third of the boardwalk on weekends. Then she told me that, believe it or not, the ocean was actually warmer in December than in the summer. That still didn't persuade me to bring my bathing trunks. She said this wasn't a real vacation, though, since she couldn't get her mind off Steven. Then she asked me if I'd gotten any letters from him. I was afraid we'd get into talking about him during our long car ride, since I wasn't sure if he'd been writing the same things to her in his letters as he was to me. I wondered if he was telling her the whole truth about his miserable situation or shielding her from some of it, especially the drugs he'd come to depend on daily.

He'd written me that he'd been rushed through Basic Training in only six short weeks. He wrote that he and his buddies from Basic were referred to by the seasoned soldiers as the "fng. Cherries," or "fucking new guys" because they'd never been under fire. He was told to "zap the gooks/dinks/slants" but never given a clear reason why. Every day, he'd learn new war words like *steel pot, spider hole,* and *fragging.* And he said that even if Vietnam did offer the novelty of two-foot long centipedes and vines that seemed to reach out and grab you only to suspend you in the air, these foreign novelties he easily could live without. He'd much rather be back home looking at the familiar landscape of New Jersey.

He already realized he'd made a mistake by not listening to Jane when she told him to burn his draft card and seek refuge in Canada. He went on to write that he knew if, and when, he had the chance to go home on leave, he'd most likely end up going AWOL.

He was never much for drugs, maybe a little pot now and then, but he found himself like a lot of the other guys who couldn't seem to make it through the day without stuff like opium, binoctal or sometimes even morphine. And the drug names also became more new words to add to his vocabulary besides offering ways to ease the depression and death that seemed to permeate everything around him.

Then there was the danger of falling into feces-smeared pits, children selling bombs disguised as ordinary looking soda cans, and "willy peter" being dumped from U.S. planes, which the soldiers were told to stay clear of because if white phosphorus could burn through steel it could burn through bone. Lastly, there was the rain that never seemed to let up and could cause "jungle rot."

Steven wrote me that he had to go through weeks or even months of this bullshit before his platoon could even think of getting any R+R, which meant he'd be having Christmas dinner in Vietnam. Anything his superiors would serve, though, had to be better than what the soldiers were forced to cook for themselves, using peanut butter and insect repellent for cooking grease. He wrote that he only hoped the troops weren't served chicken or turkey. In only three days, he'd already seen some pretty dreadful casualties. One included a soldier's entrails exposed, and he recalled that having the distinct smell of raw chicken. The experience seriously made him consider becoming a vegetarian.

I looked over at Jane as she intently watched the road, waiting for my answer as to whether Steven had written me. Since when did I become so good at keeping secrets, which went against all I'd learned from my short stint as a Catholic? And who was I really trying to protect by doing so—myself?

Not only did I keep the contents of Steven's letters from her a secret, I also didn't tell her I'd been seeing John, or that I was attracted to her, which was the real reason I chose not to mention Carl's note.

"Well?" She briefly glanced over at me, taking her eyes off the road for a second.

"Have you?" I asked, not ready to volunteer what was in my letters until she divulged what she knew first.

"Sure, I've gotten letters. He says military life's not so bad. I don't understand. Going by the news footage, Vietnam looks like hell on earth, yet he seems to be coping well. I guess my brother's a pretty strong guy, mentally. I just worry about him getting hurt or even worse, killed or dying from an overdose. I heard a lot of those soldiers are hooked on drugs. I'm glad Steven never liked them."

"He's a strong guy; I'm sure he'll be OK," I answered, all the while feeling like the despicable, deceptive secret-keeper I'd become.

"Put a tape in," Jane ordered, as she pointed to the box at my feet filled with 8-tracks.

"What do you feel like hearing?"

"I don't care. Something soothing and mindless to calm my nerves, so I don't think of Steven."

I reached down and looking for something light, grabbed the Lovin' Spoonful tape and put it in the player. I knew that the 8-track was a sort of present from Carl. He had traded some LPs with his friend, who was a car mechanic, in exchange for a new Buick Riviera 8-track player for Jane simply because he remembered her saying once that she wished her old Mercedes had come with one. Carl then had his friend install the player for her. I only hoped that she wasn't going to start talking about him. She'd already told me that she thought about Carl at least once a day since he'd left town.

Then Jane spoke over the music, "I plan on using this visit as one last mind-clearing respite before I start spring semester. I also plan to ride over to Sunset Beach in Cape May while we're there, which is only a few miles from the Wildwoods, where I want to collect some diamonds."

"Diamonds?" I asked. There's actually real diamonds on the beach?"

"They're not real diamonds but quartz crystals that come from the Upper Delaware River.

They've traveled 200 miles over thousands of years. People have been going to that beach looking for them for centuries. Native Americans always believed they brought good luck."

"So people just collect them?"

"Some do, yes. You can keep them in their natural state, which is cloudy and white, or buy a tumbler: a machine they go in and get tumbled around until they come out looking clear like diamonds. Some people also make them into jewelry."

"Then why is the place called Sunset Beach and not Diamond Beach?" I was beginning to feel like a child with all the questions.

"Because the beach is at the very tip of New Jersey, which makes sunsets over the ocean 100 percent unobscured. I've never seen it myself, but I've heard that sometimes there's this turquoise flash right before the sun sinks on the horizon."

I had been to the beaches of the Wildwoods before, whenever we'd decide to cut class, and if we felt we needed to do something more adventurous than sit in a diner or drive around for hours listening to music, but I'd never been to Cape May. I was hoping that before we left for home, I'd be able to witness one of those sunsets.

After a three-hour drive, we finally exited the Parkway and entered a whole new world of flat roads stretching out before us, dusted with a scattering of pristine sand, marsh grasses, primitive and oddly twisted holly trees, frozen custard stands, trawlers and seafood restaurants. All had been blanched by years of wind and sun, a sun that now seemed to be ferociously fighting the clouds to come out.

During the brief times that it did, it felt stronger, closer to the

Earth. I rolled down the window, even if it was winter, then I reached into the cooler in the backseat to get us two cold beers.

Soon after, we pulled into the white-pebbled driveway of the Beachcomber Hotel, a two-story square building with a modest, flickering neon sign. The place looked more like a boardinghouse or a youth hostel rather than a hotel. We grabbed our stuff from the trunk and headed to the front desk to register. The owner introduced herself and seemed like a very friendly and accommodating young woman. She held one child on her hip, while another hid behind her, as she struggled with her free hand to give us our key and registration card. Her only rule was that if we brought any music with us, like a radio or tape player, to keep the noise down after ten.

"What about room service?" I joked.

"You're looking at it," she said, as she motioned to the already darkened kitchen situated behind her and the front desk. You're welcome to use the refrigerator and stove, just please clean up after yourselves." She handed us our key, which happened to be a skeleton key, no less.

"Talk about no frills! How'd you ever find this place?" I asked Jane when we were at a distance that the woman couldn't hear. I realized at that point, as we climbed stairs to our room, that there was no elevator in sight. The hallway had a musty smell like all shore houses seem to have, only added to that was the faint smell of pot in the air.

"I didn't think anyone actually used these anymore." I said, battling with the key. As I finally got the door open, I noticed the room had only one double bed, but didn't mention the fact. I only hoped the well-worn chenille spread was free of bedbugs. Besides an old, repainted dresser, floor lamp and one wood chair, the very dusty, yellowed Venetian blinds wouldn't go up or down and were permanently closed due to a broken string. Oddly, there was no TV.

Neither of us had the ambition to unpack, so we left our no-frills hotel room and decided to take a walk on the beach that ran alongside the boardwalk. We were only 180 miles from home and yet there was no relentless rain here but no sun either. The clouds had obviously won out, yet the air felt mild for December. We walked down to the edge of the water barefoot. Jane was right, the ocean *was* actually warmer this time of year. And the beach was empty except for a few solitary old men patiently combing the sand almost grain by grain with their metal detectors. Every once in a while, one of them would bend to retrieve something and study the object, only to throw it back down again.

Jane pointed to the shells and seaweed and other stuff that had entangled itself and was caught in the coastline sea foam at our feet. "There must have been a storm here recently. A lot of this usually washes up when there's bad weather."

"What are those weird-shaped black things?"

"Egg pouches, or 'mermaid's purses'... sometimes they're called 'devil's purses.' You should see how far the ocean comes up when there's a really bad storm. I've been here when the water came out into the streets!"

Hard to believe, since the distance from where the beach began to the water's edge seemed like a half-mile trek just to get your feet wet, but then Jane told me that was because the ocean was receding each year, so Wildwood was gaining beachfront.

"I'm getting hungry," she said, suggesting we go up on the boardwalk and get something to eat."

We walked past a few piers, trying to decide on New York-style pizza or Philly cheese steaks. The cheese steaks won out. Even though Jane would be going to school in Philadelphia and could have them whenever she wanted, I rarely got the chance. New York-style pizza I could have anytime. When we finished eating, we passed an arcade that was closed. Beneath a darkening sky, we noticed a motionless gypsy fortuneteller encased in a glass box sitting in front, unable to move until summer returned. Then Jane decided instead of going back to our hotel that she wanted to stop at Douglas Fudge and buy candy. On the way to the candy shop, we passed a curious-looking, small white storefront. This time we saw a real, live fortuneteller. We found that strange, since most of the boardwalk had closed for the evening, but her door just happened to be open. She watched us as we passed, then she began motioning for us to come in, as we stopped just under the sign above her door that read *Seventh Sister-Palm Reading and Tarot.*

"Have you ever had your fortune told?" Jane wanted to know. "I'm going to ask her how much she charges and how long she takes. She looks like a real, authentic fortuneteller!"

"You mean there are real ones?" I joked, but deep down the thought made me uneasy.

"Well, compared to that animated, plastic gypsy lady in the box that we saw earlier," she said, laughing, as she pushed me in the doorway. "You go first. I'll wait out here. I'm just going to walk down to Douglas Fudge and get some candy while you're in there. I'll be right back."

"Promise?" I pleaded, as I watched her walking away.

The ancient woman put her right hand up to greet me, as I entered the cavernous room. "Sar shin," I heard her say. "Well well, look what the birds of fire have brought to this lonely old Romani—such a handsome young man." She then took me by the hand and led me through the darkened rooms. "Come in. Come in and sit down."

Before Carl left, he broke his promise: He failed in his quest to rid me of my virginity. Earlier, I'd had the opportunity to be alone with Jane in a hotel room where nothing had happened, as of yet. Now I couldn't help but wonder if I was about to be taken advantage of by a flirtatious, old gypsy woman with a gold front tooth. If so, it could possibly scar me for life. The gypsy reminded me of a spider, and I was the fly that was caught deep inside the darkness of her lair. I wanted to tell her to forget about the reading, but Jane had already wandered down the boardwalk to the fudge shop. I was all alone; there was no turning back now.

I was soon led behind faded velvet curtains, heavy with dust, to a room dimly lit by only a few flickering candles set on a table big enough for only two. The rest of the room was pitch black, but the wavering light from the candles made me wonder what presence or whose presence might also be with us, and possibly be causing just enough wind to alter their glow. All I could make out in this candlelit room was a table in the corner on which sat an antique glass lamp in the shape of a pale crescent moon with a dark red, fringed shade. I sat down, and she told me to touch the deck of tarot cards in front of me. As she spread them out, she looked at me and appeared to be analyzing my face much more than the cards. I hadn't even been in there for five minutes, and she was already telling me that I seemed to be constantly surrounded by a "mulo" or spirit, and that if it was of the evil kind could drive the living to suicide.

"Spirit?" I laughed, pretending she was telling me something I didn't already know.

"There is one mulo around you who is making himself known to you. I am seeing that he died a somewhat violent death? I can't tell if he is a good or evil mulo, but there is a reason for his visits. Are you frightened that he appears to you?"

At that moment, the hairs on the back of my neck stood up. I wasn't laughing anymore. Here I was thinking I was taking part in some harmless, bogus carney entertainment with some gold-toothed, charlatan, and she ends up knowing about John. Was this lady for real? How could she possibly know? Besides that, I don't think I was ever studied so intently by anyone before in my entire life. Even though the woman had a definite kindness that showed in her face, she had that basilisk stare that so often describes gypsies.

She kept talking, not waiting for me to answer. "Anything taken from a dead person is bad luck. I see that you have in your possession something that belongs to this spirit." She never blinked or took her eyes off me. "Since I don't know if this is a good spirit or an evil one, you must burn the object he owned at once if you want him to ever stop showing himself."

"I don't have anything of his, and we haven't been friends for years!"

"Are you sure? I see that you do. Think...there must be something! Do you have access to his grave? Go there and put stones or thornbushes around it. If you want to be safe and want this to stop, never mention his name again. Don't speak of him anymore to anyone. That is all I have to tell you for now, and I am sure that what I have said is more than enough. I don't think it would be wise to give you any more darkness than you can handle."

I sat there astounded, unable to speak or move, held by her reptilian stare. I looked down at the deck in front of me, spread out in a fan shape on the table. I finally found the courage to ask, "What card showed you that I was seeing this person I used to know...who is now dead?"

"No card; I could read everything from your face," she said, still staring. "Death does not exist; both the good and bad souls live on. I have seen that same look many times before on those like yourself, the living who are often plagued by visits from that other world—their world."

When my reading was over, I paid the gypsy and headed to the door, following her as she led me out. "Excuse me," I said, "earlier you mentioned 'birds of fire.' What are birds of fire?" Thinking they sounded like some creation conjured up in hell, I expected her to point down, but instead she pointed up toward the diamond-studded, sapphire sky. "Up there...what you call stars." Then, with her metallic smile mirroring the glint of amusement park rides, she pressed a tiny black velvet bag filled with seashells into the palm of my hand. "Keep this with you always for protection and bakt... good luck."

I found Jane sitting in front, casually eating her bag of candy. "My turn!" she said, as she quickly stood up. I grabbed her by the arm as she got to her feet and pulled her away from the storefront as fast as I possibly could. I told her to keep walking.

"What's wrong? Did she give you some bad news?"

"More creepy than bad. You know somewhere that we can sit and talk, maybe get some coffee? There's something I've been meaning to tell you, and this is as good a time as any."

We walked a few blocks to the coffee shop on Rio Grande across from the boardwalk and beach.

"Did she say something terrible like you're going to die soon?

You know they're all just fakes. I hope you don't believe her!" Jane tried to keep pace with my stride.

"She knew something she couldn't have possibly known. I freaked out and tried to convince myself that you and she must have been partners in some sort of pre-arranged charade, when you questioned her earlier out of earshot, but then I realized there was no way you could have known because I never told you."

"Never told me what? And I've never met that woman in my life."

We grabbed a small table by the window. I fidgeted with sugar packets, not knowing where to begin without having Jane think I was completely nuts. Carl—being much more open to believing in that kind of stuff—was easier to tell. We ordered two coffees and two slices of lemon meringue pie.

"Carl is the only person I ever told this to. I've been seeing John since the night he died."

I didn't realize the waitress had stopped next to our table and was standing over us ready to deliver our order, lingering much longer than she should have. I was sure it was just because she wanted to hear more of what I had to say. "Can I get you anything else?" she asked. "Thanks, I think we're good for now, but we'd like a few minutes," Jane answered, as she looked at the waitress, holding her gaze until the woman realized Jane's stare meant the woman no longer needed to be listening in on our conversation.

"What do you mean when you say that you've been seeing him?"

"Just what I said. He seems to show up a lot, especially when I'm alone."

"Does he say anything when he appears to you?"

"Not a word. He just stands there looking at me."

"That's really creepy!" Jane held herself tightly and shook as if she had a sudden chill.

"And there's something else I haven't told you. The boat came back."

"What boat?"

"You know...my boat. The one they used that night. It came

back by itself."

"What do you mean it came back by itself?"

"The very first time I saw John was the night he died. I felt so hot that night that I couldn't sleep, so I sat looking out my bedroom window. I saw this guy that looked just like John sitting on the well in my backyard. I called to him. He looked up at me, then got up and started walking away. I ran downstairs and out of the house, trying to catch up to see if it was really him. He walked downhill to the marina and to the end of the dock, then he just vanished, but there was my boat in its slip, untied."

Jane shivered again. "And what did Carl say when you told him all this?"

"You know how Carl can be. He joked around, as usual, but he did admit that he does believe in ghosts. Also, I did some work for Mrs. Kelly over the summer. I think she's been seeing John, too."

"What did she say when you told her that you've been seeing him?"

"I couldn't tell her. The whole time I was seeing him, I was hoping the visions were all in my head. I thought if I kept telling myself that it wasn't really happening, that I could make his visits stop.

After she asked me if I'd seen him—almost like she had—then I knew he wasn't in my imagination.

"So, that's why you've been acting so weird lately! Why did you wait so long to tell me?"

"Wait, there's more. Then the fortuneteller told me I'm seeing John because I have something that belongs to him, and the only way to get him to leave me alone is to burn it! I have nothing of his.

What could I possibly have? She also said she wasn't going to tell me anything else because she didn't think I could handle anything more she had to say. I'm probably going to die! She said something to the effect that if John was an evil spirit, he could haunt me until I'd most likely be driven to suicide!"

"John? An evil spirit? I don't think so." Jane laughed. "Seeing that fortuneteller was a bad idea, though. I'm sorry I ever suggested we do that. Maybe if you got out of town for a while, like I've been saying? A change of scenery? I think that might do you a world of good."

"Isn't that insane, though? I mean telling me to burn stuff? Plus, she said to go to the cemetery and put stones or thornbushes around his grave. Imagine? What would Mrs. Kelly think if she saw that? Oh, and I'm never supposed to talk about him anymore or even mention his name."

"Too late, I think we've been doing a pretty good job of that!"

I scanned the restaurant for our waitress, so we could get the check and go back to the hotel. As we walked, Jane jumped in front of me, and facing me, began to walk backwards. Trying to cheer me up and take my mind off things, she asked, "So, how do you want to ring in the new year?" I had almost forgotten it was New Year's Eve. I guess so far I hadn't been the most fun person to be around when it came to celebrating. "Well, after that fortune-telling experience earlier, I think I definitely need a few drinks. In fact, I think I need a lot of drinks!"

"Then, let's hit some bars tonight," she suggested. "What could be more appropriate than getting completely wasted? Isn't that what New Year's Eve is all about?"

We walked back to the hotel, took showers, and hit Main Street; bypassing the old man bars, we found an Irish tavern with a decent jukebox. We decided to order some appetizers with drinks, and sat at the bar until almost midnight, but I was beginning to get a little nauseated from all the pints of beer and shots of Jameson. So Jane suggested we walk to a playground on the beach where we could smoke a joint. Once there, we both took our shoes off and sat on the swings. The sand was even colder at night. I was much too dizzy to move, but as Jane pushed herself higher and higher on the swing, I watched the full moon dipping low over the ocean, illuminating a fling of tiny wintering sandpipers that almost glittered in the moonlight as they played tag with the waves at the shoreline.

As we walked back to our room, I got some spare change together, found a phone booth and decided to call home. Mom answered.

"I just wanted to wish everyone a happy new year." I had never been away from home, or even out of town for New Year's Eve before. She put my dad on first, then my grandfather, then Ike. "Will is sleeping," she said when she came back on the line. "I'll be sure to tell him that you called."

Rather than just calling to wish them a happy new year, for some reason I felt the need to call and warn them, especially Will, to make sure to be careful plugging in the Christmas tree because it had probably gotten too dry by now and could be a fire hazard. The operator came on, and I was about to be cut off. "Mom, I'm running out of change. I'll be home tomorrow." I then was forced to hang up and only hoped she or Will would have the sense not to light the dried out tree.

Back at the hotel we were both tired, cold and drunk. Jane and I lay down on the bed at the same time, next to each other like two matching bookends, while both of us stared up at the ceiling. Then Jane turned to put her head on my chest and her arm around me. "You know, I forgot to give you a kiss at midnight," she said.

"Oh yeah? How did we miss that?" I said casually, as if her kisses were an ordinary occurrence.

"We were at the playground. I kept checking my watch to see how many minutes to midnight, then I forgot until twelve o'clock passed. Besides, you were too busy looking at those sandpipers."

Nervous, I tried to steer the conversation away from where I thought it might be heading. "I was noticing the full moon; also I remember reading once that over the course of their lifetime, those tiny birds can pretty much fly that distance if they had to—from here to the moon, that is—and at speeds of 200 miles an hour!"

"That's cool!" Suddenly there was a long pause and a strained silence. "Too bad there's no TV in this place," she said.

I didn't know what she meant by that. Did she really mean that she wished there was a TV, or was there a double meaning to her words? Was she looking for another activity to pass the time? Not only did I feel awkward—a person my age who still just happened to be a virgin and just happened to be in bed with a girl—but I couldn't seem to shake the image of the ancient gypsy with the gilded tooth, and I was hoping that same image wouldn't occur to me down the road whenever I might find myself alone with a girl in the future. Still lying on my back, I turned slightly to remove the bag of shells the old woman had given me earlier that I almost forgot was still in my back pocket. Jane seemed very sleepy and asked me in a barely audible voice about what was in the bag, as I hurled it onto the top of the dresser.

"Nothing much, just a bag of shells the fortuneteller gave me for good luck. So...do you think about Carl a lot?" I decided once and for all to stop wondering if anything had ever happened between the both of them, and come right out and ask.

"Yeah, I miss him a lot. Don't you?"

"Sure, but probably not in the same way you miss him."

"What's that supposed to mean?"

"You guys seemed so close, I guess I just always assumed something was happening between the both of you. Was there...anything happening, I mean?"

"What brought this on?"

"I don't know. Correct me if I'm wrong, but didn't you always seem to have one of his shirts, a pair of his pants, or an album?"

"What girl in town didn't have something of his? No, nothing happened. He never even tried anything, and believe me, he had plenty of opportunities!" Jane sounded almost disappointed he'd never taken advantage of her.

Relieved, I stopped interrogating her as I reached my arm up without trying to move too much, and I shut off the light. I lay there awake in the dark, listening to the traffic on the streets below and the bits of conversation between the few hotel guests coming and going, all the while not afraid of seeing John, just wondering when, if, and how it would ever stop. Jane was in dreamland, unaware, but I'd been lying there so long that I noticed morning had come as slices of light from the first day of the new year, 1969, filtered through spaces between the blinds. Through the thin walls I had listened all night in the dark to music and revelers on the street. Through their facade-like flimsiness, I could even smell the fragrance of pot and incense from other rooms in our hotel, blended with the incredible scents of the bakery across the street as they made their doughnuts and pastries for the morning while everyone else had the luxury of sleep.

I could feel my eyelids finally getting heavy. I soon found myself asleep and dreaming about Will. We were both in a room I didn't recognize. We sat on a velvet couch, and we were waiting for someone or something.

Will was wearing a suit and tie but was barefoot, and there seemed to be water coming from under the couch, forming a puddle by his feet. He was sitting right next to me, but he wouldn't look at me, or talk to me. His hair appeared to be wet, as if he'd just showered. A pair of gilded frames that included very faded, boring scenes of nature adorned the wall opposite us. Below the pictures was a water fountain. Then, I woke suddenly from the dream to find Jane standing over me.

"I went across the street to the bakery and got some coffee and pastries. We should get going soon. They'll be kicking us out of here at eleven."

"I have to admit that I will seriously miss this hotel and all the luxuries it had to offer," I jested.

"I didn't want to wake you earlier. It looked like you were in the middle of a really good dream."

"Actually, I was having this weird dream about Will. We were both sitting on a couch together in a place I didn't recognize, and there was this water making a puddle under the couch by his feet. I couldn't figure out where all the water was coming from. He wouldn't say a word to me, just kept staring straight ahead."

"I guess then I didn't miss a visit from John while I was asleep?"

She obviously didn't seem too concerned about helping me analyze my dream. "No. Maybe the bag of shells kept him away," I joked but secretly hoped it was true.

We both downed the coffee and pastries, then checked out. Our only plans had been to drive over to Sunset Beach and collect

Jane's "diamonds" before we hit the Parkway for home, a three hour drive without traffic. Our last day in Wildwood and even though I was glad to leave that hotel, I wasn't so glad to get back to my routine. Who was I kidding? What routine? Everyone else, including Carl, seemed to have one. The time had come when I'd finally have to give some serious thought as to what I planned to do with my life. I realized I was desperately needed at the marina now that I'd graduated, but John's *death* had changed my *life*. I couldn't understand why he chose me. Maybe Jane was right, I needed to get out of town, even if it was only temporary. Maybe by leaving Pleasant Valley I'd leave his spirit behind, too.

I told Jane that after we left the beach, if she didn't mind dropping me at the Wildwood station, that I didn't mind taking a bus home, which would leave me off in New York City right across the bridge. That would mean catching one more bus to town from there. But Jane insisted on driving me all the way back to Pleasant Valley since her parents would be returning from St. Maarten, and she wanted to stop in and wish them both a happy new year anyway. Besides, she assured me, she had to get some things she'd forgotten when first moving to her school.

On the way to Sunset Beach, we drove on country roads passing meadows on either side, then roads lined with beach grass, and bare-branched oak and poplar trees. I imagined them not so long ago, lush and green, now they stood in melancholy shades of tan and gray looking more like they had been parched in a recent fire rather than victims in the grip of yet another funereal East Coast winter. In the distance, the tall, stately lighthouse stood proud and fearless, like all lighthouses, weathering decades of harsh seasons and the unforgiving storms that come with them.

The sun felt warm on my face when we got out of the car. Besides two other cars, we were the only ones parked in the beach lot. I didn't know what to expect when we got there. When Jane had first said that diamonds were on the beach, I imagined traffic backed up in all directions leading to it, while crowds of beach-goers already there were filling their buckets with precious stones and fighting to the death over them as they washed onto the shore. I'd wondered why I'd never heard of this place in the past, this free-access beach that could make anyone and everyone instantly rich. I knew that they weren't real but was still curious to see what all the fuss was about, what they looked like in their natural state, and why anyone would want to collect them.

I was surprised to find the sand so coarse and dark compared with the Wildwoods, whose beachfront was almost like fine, white powder. We walked slowly on the sand while Jane, like an expert, carefully studied stones that had been brought in with the tide.

"What is that out there sticking up out of the water?" I pointed to something that looked like a tremendous pile of half-submerged rock.

"That's the *Atlantus*, one of twelve experimental concrete ships built for our military during World War I. The fleet wasn't ready in time, not until the war had been over for a month, so rather than completely waste them, they got put to use transporting our troops home from Europe."

"How did the thing sink?"

"After the war, the ship sat for six years until a man bought her intending to use her as a passenger ferry, but she was never put into commission because there was a bad storm that caused her to break free from her mooring, and it ran aground off the coast."

"Why would anyone want to make a ship out of concrete?"

"My dad's version is that there was a shortage of steel at the time. The military needed something impenetrable and strong to protect themselves from the German U-boats. I've heard the soldiers feared more for their lives having to be transported all the way across the Atlantic in one of those things than the battlefields they'd survived! They called them 'floating tombstones,' and they were even more afraid when they saw bags of cement being stored on board for repairs in case they might happen to hit something which could cause a major crack, as this had already happened to some of the rest of the fleet. Can you imagine?"

Impressed, I questioned her, "How do you know all this?"

"My dad was obsessed! Every summer when we came to Wildwood, I had to listen to him tell the same story over and over to anyone who would care to listen, including strangers on the beach."

The pebbles that washed up with each wave didn't look all that different from one another, but Jane seemed to be able to sort the quartz from the rest by holding bunches of the rounded, cloudy stones in her hands and letting water run through them to rinse the sand off. When she was satisfied with her catch, I asked, "Now what? They don't look much like diamonds to me. How do you get them to turn clear?"

"Come on, I'll show you." Then she pointed to the tiny wood shack on the beach that was a gift shop. "Over there." she said, while putting what she had collected into a plastic bag. We walked over to the small wooden building but noticed that even though the lights were on, there was a "closed" sign hanging on the door. We looked in the window and saw a middle-aged, gray-haired woman wearing glasses, taking items out of a showcase and studying them carefully as she wrote. We knocked on the door, but the woman ignored us and continued writing. Jane gave one last try by tapping on a window pane. The woman became visibly annoyed but then removing her glasses finally looked up at us. She came over to the door and unlocked it. Without opening it fully, she said through the small crack, "Can't you read the sign awn the door? We're closed. " in that southern New Jersey dialect, so different from those of us who lived up north.

"Happy New Year!" said Jane, trying to soften the woman. "Sorry to bother you, but my friend and I have come a long way, and he was curious to see what the actual diamonds look like after they've been tumbled and cut. I promise, if you let us in, that we won't take up a lot of your time." The woman sighed loudly. "You'll have to be quick. I'm taking inventory and wasn't planning on being here for too long myself today. I'm going to lock the door behind you. I don't want anyone else thinking I'm open."

"Thanks! We promise we won't be long." Jane then steered me over to some glass showcases. She pointed downward and inside to a display of necklaces, rings and earrings, all mounted with Cape May diamonds. In their polished state, they actually were hard to tell them from the real thing.

"How long does the process take to get them to look this way?"

"They have to be tumbled for at least seven days in one of those machines."

"Seems like a lot of bother for one stone when the store sells them already polished. Why not just buy them here finished or go buy zircons? Wouldn't that save a lot of time and work?"

The woman remained behind the counter. Ignoring us, she continued to take inventory, as if we weren't there.

"But this gives me a sense of satisfaction to know I really made something."

"Do you even have one of these machines?"

"There's one at my house that I'll pick up when we get back to Pleasant Valley. My dad bought the machine for me a while ago, but I'm sure it still works."

After making the woman open the shop for us, we both felt guilty for having interrupted her work only to leave without buying anything. At that point, I thought of buying Jane one of the "diamonds" already set in a piece of jewelry as a token of our New Year's weekend we'd spent together but realized she might take that the wrong way, so I didn't even suggest it.

She spotted a paperback about Cape May ghosts. "This book looks interesting. What do you think? Should I get it?" She laughed to herself, as she studied the cover. "This book is actually supposed to be nonfiction. Then she said, surprised, "Sorry!" I assumed her apology was for thinking she might have offended me for making fun of the fact that ghosts could be real.

"Go ahead and get it. I've got enough of my own ghosts to contend with. I don't feel a need to read about anybody else's ghosts. Wait, let me buy the book for you." I felt for my wallet in my jeans pocket and realized then that I didn't have the bag of shells the gypsy woman had given me for good luck. I must have left them back on the hotel dresser.

"No. That's OK, you don't have to do that."

"I know I don't have to, but I want to. Damn! I left that bag of shells back at the hotel!"

"Do you want to go back for them?"

"No, no big deal. I'm sure that was all Gypsy mumbo jumbo anyway." But when Jane didn't offer to drive back to the hotel a second time, I knew I'd be forced to leave them there, forever wondering if they would maybe have had the power to keep John away.

The woman behind the counter who'd been ignoring us, writing and taking inventory the whole time, her eyes following us around, eavesdropped with that same look the waitress had in the coffee shop the day before. Then she finally said, "Are you folks about ready? I'd really like to close soon." I paid her for the book, thanked her, and we headed for home.

The Piper at the Gates of Dawn

Lying there looking out my window, I thought of Jane back at school. Almost a week had passed, and I guessed she was probably still tumbling her rocks. I looked down at the small pile of albums on my bedroom floor that Carl had left me, the only ones he could salvage as he ran to escape the walls that were coming down around him. I thought of him and Steven, each surrounded by palm trees, but one in the heaven that I'd always imagined to be California and the other in what I could only imagine to be the hell that was Vietnam.

The wind moaned as it whipped around the house again, passing my room each time and leaving behind the coldest chill as it shook and rattled the panes of the drafty old windows, a wind that sounded almost angry not to be able to get inside. I pulled the covers up higher. I could see a hawk circling the sky above the Palisades. I hoped the bird's intermittent cries would lull me back to sleep, but since John's death sleep hadn't come easy for me.

In a kind of half-sleep, I was imagining the faint sounds of what sounded like sirens of fire engines. When they seemed to be getting much closer, I knew then that they were real. Will's room was at the other end of the hall. I debated whether or not to wake him. I found him sitting in bed, rambling that the Captain warned him to avoid fire. With my mom, dad and grandfather on their way to Canada for a few days, Ike stayed behind to help at the marina, but he didn't live with us, so Will's safety was my sole responsibility. Despite his faith in the Captain, I was forced to have Will come outside with me so I could see where the fire was and if it posed any danger to us, rather than leave him at the house where he might be alone and frightened.

We dressed quickly. As we ran down the lane, following the sirens of fire engines coming one after another we saw that the marina was what was on fire! Horrified, we watched sparks while they did a teasing sort of dance as they flew up from the burning dock to the trees on the cliffs behind us. I saw a number of New York water boats already coming across the river to help, as well as fire trucks from surrounding towns that sat on the cliffs above us. Firemen were everywhere.

"What happened?" I screamed at Ike over all the commotion.

"Someone's Christmas tree caught fire!" he yelled, gesturing up toward a building on the forested Palisades behind us. "See that apartment house? Everything went up from one tree. The wind carried sparks down here through the woods, and now they're blowing back up there again.

The firemen are trying to contain the flames on both ends. Let's hope we don't lose this place, especially under my watch, with your grandfather and parents not here! You and Will need to keep safe. Stay out of the way, especially of the gas docks, and let the firemen do their work."

"OK. I'll take Will back to the house." Even though I wanted to help in the worst way, my eyes were burning in the short time I'd been there, and I didn't want to admit that breathing had become pretty difficult from all the smoke.

I was concerned for Ike. He wasn't young anymore. When he was no longer in sight, I defied him. I felt so helpless watching the firemen trying to manage the weight of water from the hoses that I attempted to help them hold one up. At that moment I saw my brother propelled into the air, as he accidentally stepped into the path of the stream of water and was instantly knocked off the dock by its force. When I looked again, he was gone. I yelled for help. Not waiting to see if anyone had heard me, I jumped in to find him. With all the confusion and noise going on around the marina, no one had seemed to notice that Will had gone in the water except for one other fireman who quickly removed his protective gear and jumped in not too far from where I had. The frantic fear I was feeling made it hard to hold my breath for long underwater. I opened my eyes, and the water was such a thick gray-green that was impossible to see in. Blindly thrashing around as I felt for any sign of him, I was choking from holding my breath underwater, but when I could no longer hold it and came up, I was choking from breathing in the burning air above the water as the strong gusts of wind blew pieces of black wood and embers into my face. I also noticed that I had to get out of the current, since it was rapidly pulling me away from the marina. With all my strength, I tried to swim to shore, as far away from the burning dock as my exhausted body could manage. A painful, almost paralyzing cramp shot up my back as I tried to fight the direction the river was dragging me. Finally, I reached the shoreline, where I crawled to a place in the thick mud and reeds. As an ember storm swirled all around me, and a wall of relentless fire danced in front and behind, I sat trying to catch my breath, while I helplessly watched the lone fireman still in the water, searching frantically. I watched others on shore, watched the black smoke and angry flames make their way to the gas docks, watched the sparks being carried by the dry winter wind, and I realized then that I didn't care if the entire marina blew up, I just wanted my brother found alive.

***

I felt both strange and awkward having to hold Will's clothes on my lap, as I waited with my mom and dad in the reception area of the funeral home. Sitting there, I thought how strange that we'd be asked to bring an outfit to be cremated or buried in right down to the shoes, socks and underwear, like he was actually going someplace. We decided he'd wear his only suit and his favorite tie; the same one he had worn to John's funeral not so long ago.

For forty-five minutes the staff had ignored us, until finally a man approached and introduced himself as the mortician. We were then led into a room adorned with cheap, cheesy silk plants covered in dust, a matching printed sofa with chairs; dull, nondescript paintings like those seen in medical offices, and numerous tissue boxes strategically placed on dark wood end tables. Going by the lack of attention we'd received so far, the tissues must have been placed around the room to relieve the staff of having to dole out even the slightest amount of compassion or consolation.

After just getting us seated, the mortician excused himself yet again to check on the validity of my brother's life insurance policy, while I took notice of my surroundings. Having a dreaded feeling of déjà vu, I began to realize just where I'd seen this tacky, wood-paneled room before, and I knew why this place felt so oddly familiar. A sudden chill went through me, as I remembered that this was the same room as in my dream, the one where Will and me are sitting on a couch, but he won't look at me.

My dad must have noticed that I was looking a little peaked because he quickly got my mom and me some water from the nearby fountain, which I remembered was also in my dream.

"Are you OK?" my dad asked. "Suddenly you look very pale."

"I'm fine." I answered, realizing my vision was a warning that had sadly come true, as I noticed my mom just sitting there, staring out the window, oblivious to our conversation.

I forced myself into thinking Will was at home waiting for us. The whole thing seemed so surreal. I wished the dream I had just weeks before hadn't been so vague. Maybe I would have made Will stay at the house the day of the fire, whether that meant him being alone or not. For that reason alone, I realized I would always feel that I was to blame for his death. Why hadn't I listened to Ike when he told us to keep out of the way?

When the mortician returned, he brought with him some barely warm coffee in tiny Styrofoam cups along with little wooden stirrers and some packets of sugar and creamer. He impatiently flung these on the coffee table in front of us, while every few minutes he would either check the time, admire his expensive watch, or both. He offered all the options. His mannerisms and method were beginning to make me feel like we were meeting with a used car salesman. My mom thought about cremation. Even though the Catholic Church was against that, she didn't care what they considered to be right or wrong since they were always changing the rules anyway. What she knew for sure was that she didn't want the church involved in any part of Will's service. In the end, she was left with burning him or putting him in the frozen ground. If she had decided on cremation, I thought how ironic it would be to have escaped fire by drowning only to succumb to it again later. No earthly ritual would be a comfort to her or us. By the time we left, the three of us had settled on a graveside ceremony.

***

I woke to find myself on the couch in the living room with Fritz by my side, his head in my lap, and so early in the morning that the test pattern was still on TV. Pain from my violent headache meant that at least I was still alive, which was more than I could say for Will.

Last night, wanting to be alone, I had hidden myself in the basement. And as I sat there for hours on the stone floor, I managed to polish off an entire bottle of vodka from my parent's stash. I had hoped that the liquor would help me to wake from this nightmare, but sadly the nightmare was real. Nauseous and dizzy, I forced myself off the couch to dress for Will's funeral, getting up slowly to turn off the TV as a nervous and confused Fritz jumped down off the couch and followed my every move.

Passing by the bay window, I stopped to look out at the river. It seemed every memory of us growing up together, not only as brothers but as friends, came crashing back. I closed my eyes and could picture Will in front of me, chubby and freckled with light brown hair, his blue eyes and fair complexion probably inherited from the Irish on my mom's side. Regarding myself, I was said to have been too thin by some. I not only had a dark complexion but also dark hair and eyes, most likely from the German on my dad's side. You'd never know looking at us that we were once brothers. We were once brothers. I got chills when I realized I'd have to refer to us in the past tense for the rest of my life.

Will always had an easygoing temperament and never got riled, unless of course, his food items would happen to touch one another on his plate. After years of listening to him complain, Mom finally had the idea of getting him a blue plate so that each serving would be in its own separate section.

Those were the uncomplicated years, though, when time seemed to move at a steady pace. With only a year between us, we were both equals because we shared the same interests. Then came the years when I would slowly start surpassing him as I welcomed the milestones, those familiar, expected and anticipated rites of passage for all teenagers. I think that's why Mom got Fritz. Not that the dog would ever take the place of me as a brother or friend to Will, but maybe just to serve as a distraction from my becoming an adult. I would be of legal age to drink and drive, while time would abruptly come to a standstill for Will, and he'd forever remain a child. But then, he always seemed to be not only blind to rites of passage, but to the passage of time itself, especially when time influenced fashion.

The Beatles' haircuts, which were considered inappropriate not so long ago, now seemed short compared to the new hairstyles of 1968. Before the Beatles, American males were forced to look—or chose to look—like plastic Ken dolls that had just broken free from their packaging and sprung to life.

Will had no problem continuing that tradition with his tucked-in, short-sleeved, button-down shirts, high-waisted pants with belt, and regular trips to the barber.

His favorite holiday, even more than Christmas, was Halloween. I think my dad's love of horror movies and science fiction shows had rubbed off on us. Usually my dad would turn all the lights off in the living room, while we sat and watched shows like *Thriller*, *One Step Beyond*, *The Twilight Zone*, or *The Outer Limits*. Will also loved the movie *House on Haunted Hill* with Vincent Price, but he didn't love the house in town that reminded him so much of the one used in the film. Most days we ran right past it, except for Halloween when we both had to admit that, like most kids in town, that particular Pleasant Valley house seemed like the perfect gothic spectacle— the perfect place to trick or treat. Dressed in our costumes, we'd ring the bell, step back from the doorway, and then run for our lives before anyone would even answer the door.

When Will and I were young, part of our summers were spent escaping to cabins on a lake in Ontario. Our grandfather was a member of the American Canoe Association at the time, and would row all the way up from Pleasant Valley to the club's privately owned land, Sugar Island, which the Association purchased in 1901. Located a hundred miles north of Syracuse, the island was one of the Thousand Islands that belong to the Canadian side and include thirty-five miles of primitive forest, coves and trails.

Sometimes our grandfather would go with Ike, sometimes with my dad. We'd drive up to meet them. The cabins where we stayed surrounded a lake so clear that, close to shore, you could see all the way to the bottom. He would take Will and me out in his canoe to the middle, and teach us to read the water. He'd tell us that navigating water was a lot like driving a car when you always have to keep an eye on the road ahead of you, so that you'd have the chance to react to obstacles. He also said you should know the body of water's age since they all have different characteristics. The young could have waterfalls and steep drops, while the old were the most easy to navigate, and the middle-aged usually had features of both. He said that pressure and obstacles, like rocks under water, created waves and should be avoided. There were also eddies and v-tongues. Eddy-hopping could be used to your advantage to temporarily stop your boat and give you time to make decisions about obstacles that might be ahead. Weather had to be paid attention to since it affected the behavior of the water. And also color: the darker the water, the deeper; the lighter, the more shallow and the more cautious you should be.

To keep us occupied some nights around the lakeside cabin, my mom would give us sparklers, and Will and I would run through the dark while they hissed and sizzled, waving them around as we drew pictures that seemed to freeze momentarily on the black night air.

The rest of our summers were spent tolerating the heat and humidity of Pleasant Valley. The only relief our yard had to offer was the sprinkler, which we'd also use to fill our water pistols. The fact that we lived in a shady lane helped a little, although if you've ever witnessed a humid summer in New Jersey, you know the shade doesn't really help much at all. Across from our house was a large grassy lot overrun with strawberries, sweet pea, and tiger lilies in summer. An old wooden arbor held wild riverbank grape; the vines, twisting as they consumed its underlying wood frame made the place great for hide and seek. Summer nights were like traveling through our own infinite twinkling galaxy, as we collected lightning bugs in jars our mom saved for us. We'd punch holes in the metal lids and make beds out of blades of grass for the jar bottoms only to find out by morning that, though we intended to be kind, we had suffocated most of them. Feeling like murderers, we'd set the few survivors free.

On the lot sat an old, abandoned barn-like shed with a loft, serving as the perfect vehicle for a young boy's imagination. The weathered wood shack would have made a terrific clubhouse had the boys from the streets nearby been allowed to wander from home and play in the lane. There was only one boy who played with us there and that was John since he lived next door. I guess the three of us could have formed a club, but a club with just three members seemed pointless.

The only condition Mrs. Kelly set for John was to make him promise that he'd get back home every day before his dad got home from work, since his dad forbade him to ever leave the yard. John was constantly being punished for one thing or another. As punishment, he was either made to do chores or forced to sit outside on a chair for hours at a time. Our yards were separated by a wooden fence with a section where it got low enough so he could make a quick dash back and forth between them to make a sudden escape, should we hear his dad's car coming up the lane. Some days, he wasn't so lucky when he couldn't get home fast enough. Now, not only was John gone but Will, too.

Fritz whimpered and brought me back to reality, and I reminded myself that the limo would be here soon. I had to get dressed quickly. I looked down at him and patted him on the head. "I know you miss Will. So do I." He gazed up at me and tilted his head to one side, trying to dissect every word.

For What It's Worth

Almost a year had gone by since Will died. I had never remembered feeling so alone before. He was gone. Carl was gone. Steven and Jane were gone. The October before last, when I felt like our little world might be changing in a bad way, I had no idea just how much. I had become reclusive and depressed, wanting to shut out the world. No longer interested in food, alcohol had become my new habit. I found myself drinking every day, and the time of day didn't seem to matter either. Even though there was a liquor store in town, most days I'd find myself walking to one on the other side of the George Washington Bridge, constantly fighting the steel stucture's magnetic lure: the silent invitation for me to stop and look down. Every day I would stop right in the spot John had stood before he jumped, the line where one state ended and the other began. Ignoring the sound of the thunderous traffic behind me, the car tires humming as they made contact with the contracting steel, first I'd look to my left and see the immense, colorless skyline of Manhattan, then to my right at the equally immense and colorless cliffs of the Palisades dotted with branchless trees and tiny houses here and there. I'd dare myself to look down at the swift current of the churning, gray-green river. Then I'd walk to a liquor store in Washington Heights just on the other side of the bridge, and since I never seemed to be able to sleep anymore, I'd arrive there pretty early, usually just when they'd open. I'd buy a pint of vodka a day to keep in my coat pocket, so I always had some with me wherever I went, which if I wasn't with Fritz, was usually by myself. If I was held under the same spell as most of the town seemed to be, it was understandable.

I guessed I wasn't the only one trying to escape reality. I had been reading Steven's letters about what army life was like and no matter how hard I tried, I didn't have the energy to answer them. I was surprised to read that the military turned their heads when it came to any drug use other than marijuana.

He had written in the past that the soldiers got and used whatever hard drugs they wanted—himself included—but not marijuana, since marijuana possession equaled a court-martial. For all other drugs, the top brass turned their backs and pretended they didn't see. Some of the drugs were even bought from children, and all were easy to get and cheap. I was shocked to hear him admit that besides pot there were weeks when he'd buy anything that was offered. He said they were the only way he could cope; he preferred, like the others, to be "out of it" most of the time. All along he'd written Jane different letters about how everything was going well, or at least as well as could be expected given the circumstances. But then he'd write me to promise not to tell Jane about his new vice—Steven, who never had a vice. Considering where he was, he certainly deserved one vice, if not many...vices that, judging from what he'd seen of war, would probably be with him for life. He wrote that he'd witnessed things firsthand he wished he could forget, like the bottom half of his close friend's body being blown off after he accidentally stepped on a land mine as he tried to save someone else. The army told the deceased soldier's parents that because of their son's bravery the soldier would be buried with honors at Arlington. His mother refused, wanting nothing more to do with the military and its senseless war; her one and only son would be buried in the family plot.

Jane was living full time on campus in Philadelphia, and she was two months into her fall semester. Before Will died and before the fire, we would call each other and talk on the phone pretty frequently, but like writing, I had no energy for making phone calls anymore either; and even though I wanted to more than anything, I didn't dare mention Steven's new habit. What good would that do him or her? If I were in his shoes—and I realized I could be at any time—I'd probably do the same thing to get through each day. She already knew about the rampant drug use among American soldiers and mentioned once that she realized the chance of him being killed in combat wasn't all that she had to worry about. He had taken her advice and gotten out of the "hole" that was Pleasant Valley but somehow had managed to get himself into an even deeper one.

I decided to get out of the house. Wandering aimlessly, I took Fritz with me as we walked briskly up to the site where Carl used to live. I was surprised to find that there was no trace of the small, ancient cemetery or stone staircase, no trace of the running stream or majestic trees, no wisteria, no house—just dirt, concrete and rebar. Even the last lonesome gargoyle was gone. It was as if Carl and the Castle were something I'd imagined, something that never existed.

Only the second week of November but going by how the trees in town looked, fall was long gone. They all seemed to share my sentiment, looked depressed, gloomy and forlorn; their once vibrant foliage replaced only by the starkness of bare black branches outlined in an early snow. I didn't want to let go of the season that had passed. If I were granted one wish, it would be the power to stop time because I knew as time went on, there would be months, then years, separating me from Will.

From the construction site we walked down to the cemetery. On the way, we passed a homeless person begging for change. In an indirect way the poor and homeless made me think of Carl, not that Carl was homeless, but he was out there in all that sunshine, and a much less harsh place to be if you were ever forced to live without a roof over your head. I dug deep into my pockets and pulled out a few quarters, feeling much closer to God by dropping them into this man's palm than I'd ever felt dropping them into the many church collection baskets I'd come across in the past.

We cut through the Veteran's Field where a flock of geese, taking a rest from the long journey ahead of them, stood pecking at the unmelted patches of snow on the ground. Fritz barked frantically as he ran up to them. They weren't the least bit bothered as they stopped briefly to look at him, but kept right on with what they were doing as if he wasn't there. He suddenly became quiet and glanced up at me with a quizzical look, probably wondering why they didn't fear him the same way the seagulls usually would.

"You can't scare them," I said. "They're almost the same size as you!"

Just a few more blocks and we were at the cemetery. Fritz and I visited almost every day. He always seemed to know where Will was buried and would run ahead looking back at me. He'd bark every time, as if to say, "Hurry up, over here."

I remember the day of Will's funeral, riding behind the hearse as it slowly made its way through the iron gates and up the path to the cemetery. With the ground being too weak to support the cars, we'd have to walk part of the way. My dad and I walked on either side of my mom, holding her up.

The clouds hung motionless in the sky that day. No birds sang, including the cardinal that solemnly watched us from an ancient oak. There was no wind, no bells echoing from across the Hudson. As we were led to folding chairs under a tent, it was as if I were someone else from another life, suspended in time, stuck in the landscape of some muted watercolor painting that was totally foreign to me, one I desperately wanted to escape. Back at the house, I quickly dodged family and friends that were standing amid the thick fog of cigarette smoke, as well as generously donated food and drink, all of which made me nauseous, family and friends included. After I'd overheard some quietly saying that it was a blessing in disguise that Will was gone, since he could only be a burden, I thought they seemed as if they were discussing some useless, damaged, imperfect piece of furniture that would be better off discarded. I remember then that I climbed the stairs and opened the door to Will's room. Like time hadn't moved forward, everything was where Will had put it since the day of the fire, and my mom had every intention of keeping it just as he'd left it. I found Fritz on Will's bed chewing on a wooden spoon he must have stolen from the dining room buffet table. I remember that he'd stopped what he was doing and gave me a look to say he knew what I was doing, too, since he also was there to escape everyone, as well as our recent, unimaginable reality.

I sat on a bench near Will's grave and watched hungry sparrows as they searched for food on the ground. I remember how Will always felt so sorry for the ones in our yard having to be outside in the cold that he'd throw them pieces of bread from our kitchen window. Once, when the wind had rustled some dry leaves lifting them off the ground, I'd sworn I'd heard his voice; Fritz even seemed to notice. Snow began to fall. Funny how something that fell so soft and quiet could be so deafening in its silence. As the thick snowflakes came down, I lifted my face to study the shapes as they floated in slow motion toward me.

I took comfort in knowing that my brother wasn't a stranger to this cemetery. I knew the Captain was here, and for what it was worth, John, too. I wondered why the Captain had never appeared to me. Would he show himself now? Would Will? Why was it just John that I always ever saw? I took the pint out of my pocket and downed the whole thing quickly. I seemed to be thinking about death and the dead a lot lately. I thought about all those who doubted there was a god, or some all-knowing, astral presence, the same ones who thought that life on Earth was the result of some giant scientific accident that just happened by chance. All nature, all galaxies, the whole universe in its perfection, all just one big mistake with death being the end and nothing else beyond. I couldn't say which side was right, the ones who believed in heaven and hell, or the ones who believed that existence ended with life on Earth; but with no proof on either side, both seemed pretty adamant in their beliefs. I wasn't one of those who believed we were a cosmic mistake and that death was the end. If that were the case—that there was nothing else—then why was life so short and death so long? A man's life, as we knew it, was measured in years, and sometimes, but rarely, a century—while death was forever.

**

Now that the boating season had ended, I was spending my afternoons trying to finish the repairs and painting I'd started at Mrs. Kelly's last winter, since I was usually needed at the marina full time every April to the first of November. When Mrs. Kelly asked if I wanted a radio to keep me company as I painted the upstairs bedrooms, I asked if she would mind instead if I brought some of Carl's albums he gave me. She said she didn't mind and that I could use John's old turntable. I found the painting to be cathartic since the repetitive task gave me time to be alone with my thoughts while I listened to music. And I could easily get away with drinking the vodka, keeping the pint out of sight whenever she'd check on how I was doing but taking it out often to maintain a constant buzz, hoping I'd never come down. I didn't think she'd mind, though, since I'd caught her once or twice when I went to rinse paintbrushes in the basement sink as I'd pass the kitchen, and she'd be pouring whiskey into her tea but didn't realize I'd seen her.

As I painted, I remembered the dream I had about Will and John in my boat as they rowed away from the marina. I had to wonder if the gypsy woman was right. Maybe John was an evil spirit, or "mulo," and the dream was his way of telling me that he was going to take my brother from me. I thought of the fortuneteller not wanting to tell me more than I could handle. I also remember her saying that when we dream of the dead, they're attempting to cross over from their world to communicate some message from beyond the grave. I thought of Carl then, joking about the very same thing.

I'd also been doing Mrs. Kelly the favor of picking up her groceries, since she had become practically agoraphobic, never setting foot outside the front door, even to get the mail, which I brought in when I came every afternoon. I was probably the only person she'd seen since my brother's funeral, of which she chose only to attend the cemetery and not our house afterwards.

Most nights, she'd beg me to stay for dinner, even though I had no interest in food. "Nothing fancy," she'd say. "I'm just so tired of having only the TV to talk to at night."

Some nights I'd stay, and we'd play cards or watch Dean Martin or Ed Sullivan. When she'd excuse herself to make her tea in the kitchen, I'd take the vodka from my pocket. Sadly, this was what my social life had become: spending my time alone with Fritz or a lonely old widow who, like myself, had lost someone that she would have easily given her own life for without a second thought.

***

The walls and old wooden windows in both the upstairs bedrooms were in bad shape and needed a lot of prep work. When I was finally finished prepping, and it was time to prime the walls, I moved to the side of the room first that faced the river. From the window, I could see the giant ice floes below in the freezing Hudson creeping slower than the clouds that were reflected in the sky above them.

Disraeli Gears was on the turntable, and I had the volume turned up pretty high when I thought I heard footsteps coming up the hall stairs. I knew it couldn't be Mrs. Kelly since I was used to the sound of her walking around the house by then, even the way she'd walk up the stairs when she'd check on me. This was definitely more like a man's footsteps, and they seemed to stop on the top landing right outside the doorway where I was working. I stayed facing the window, expecting John's ghost, but chose to ignore the sound and keep painting. I took another sip of vodka, and as soon as I put the bottle down, I could feel that the presence had entered the room, which moved very close behind me. I braced myself when I heard a voice directly in my right ear, no more than a whisper. It sang along with Jack Bruce to the record on the turntable. I turned quickly to my right then, but when I looked over my shoulder, this blur of a person, with what appeared to be dark wings for arms had already shifted to the left, behind me.

Afraid to turn around, I did so very slowly, and found it wasn't John but Carl. I just stared at first then reached my hand out and touched him to see if he was real.

"Your mom said I'd find you here. Yeah, it's me. I'm back, man."

I grabbed him and hugged him so hard. Then, the tears that I'd been holding back for so long since Will died, came rushing out, and I had no control over them; they wouldn't stop.

"I'm so sorry to hear about your brother. Why didn't you let me know? You never answered my note. Did you even get the package I sent him?"

I moved over to the turntable and shut it off. "I wanted to tell you. I didn't know where to reach you. There was no address on the inside note, and I was unable to read anything on the package because of all the rain we had."

"Well, I'm back...for good."

"I'm so glad! But I thought you said the vibe was changing here?"

"The vibe was too heavy there, that whole Manson thing. And...I guess what they say is true."

"What do they say?"

"That you might be able to take the person out of Pleasant Valley, but you can never take Pleasant Valley out of the person."

I laughed, as I wiped my tears on the sleeve of my sweatshirt.

For the next half hour, Carl in his fringed suede jacket, the one I mistook for evil angel wings, picked up a paintbrush to help me finish priming the walls. But with the sky growing dark and making things hard to see, I told him that I should stop for the day. He helped me get things cleaned and put away, and then I told Mrs. Kelly I wouldn't be staying for dinner that night and hoped she wouldn't mind. She said she understood that Carl and I had a lot of catching up to do.

We decided to head straight for the Lookout to have some drinks and talk about all the things that had gone on in the past year. When I took the empty pint from my pocket and dumped it in a trash can along the way, Carl asked what was up with the vodka.

"I don't know. I'm starting to think my sudden love for alcohol might be some Lenape curse."

"What?" he said, laughing, but so unlike Carl, I sensed a new solemn sadness about him.

We found two seats at the bar even though the place was already crowded.

"I thought for sure you'd stay in California with all that nice weather. Winter's not even here yet, and we've already had our first snowstorm."

"I guess I just missed seeing the river and being close to it. Have you heard how Jane is doing?"

"She should be home on winter break in a few weeks."

"And Steven?"

"He's coping—barely. He wrote me that since combat is so horrific, he's doing a ton of drugs just to get by."

"Are you serious? He'd be the last person I'd expect to do drugs, no matter what the situation."

Before I could say more, Lenny noticed us and came over to take our order. "It's so good to see you guys! Where have you been hiding? I was afraid they'd shipped you off to the war!"

"Nobody's shipping this guy anywhere!" Carl said then he told Lenny he'd been living in California for the past year. I added that I'd just been doing stuff around town.

"Keeping a low profile, huh? How are your parents doing?" Lenny asked me.

"They're getting by. Taking it a day at a time. Have Dunn and Hale been here?"

"Haven't seen them. Don't care to either." Lenny answered just as someone was trying to get his attention. He had to excuse himself and walked away to get their drinks.

"What a terrible tragedy that was with your brother, man." Carl shook his head while looking down. "Your mom told me they were in Canada when the accident happened. And how days before the fire Will had told her the Captain said to be careful. She'll never forgive herself for not listening."

"Yeah...same here. None of us ever paid attention to the Captain." We both sat there drinking for a while, neither one of us knowing what to say next to break the sudden, uncomfortable silence.

"So have you been up to see my old home or what's left of it?"

"The Castle? Everything's gone! Someone even managed to rip off that last gargoyle!"

"Damn! Those things must have been so heavy. I could never figure out how anyone got away with them, unless they walked off by themselves. And they always seemed to get stolen at night."

Hoping Carl would explain the reason for his sad and serious behavior that was certainly out of character and that took some getting used to, I decided to pry him. "So tell me about California. From what you wrote, you had a rough time getting there?"

"Yeah, I wrote you about getting ripped off and stranded by that truck driver, right? And that old waitress letting me crash at her place for the night? Then I was lucky enough to bum a ride from those girls with the van."

I waited for him to bring up the girl who he thought he might be in love with.

"When I got to California, at first I felt displaced and homesick. I realized being in a canyon and not near the river when you're used to that can be kind of claustrophobic. But the place actually turned out to be pretty cool...at least for a while. I told you about Marina, that girl I met? We ended up having a lot of the same friends." Then Carl let out a deep sigh.

"What happened with that? Are you planning to keep in touch? You think she'll ever come here to visit?"

Carl looked down and mumbled, "No, she's dead, murdered. They found her body on New Year's Day not far from where I was staying. The cops actually came looking for me because they found a photo of me in her purse." Then Carl looked up at me teary-eyed and laughed to himself. I told her I once lived in a castle here. Marina thought the idea of castles in New Jersey was pretty funny and unbelievable, so she started calling me The King of Jersey, even wrote it in marker on the Polaroid the cops were convinced they had as evidence against me. Anyway, after a lot of questioning and my friends vouching for my whereabouts the night of the murder, the fuzz finally let me go."

I sat there stunned, but I knew Carl wasn't capable of murder. "How was she killed?"

"Hundreds of stab wounds. At first the place was like paradise. Everyone knew each other, so we all kept our doors unlocked. I got to meet a lot of well-known musicians who lived there. I'd go to their houses or the clubs on Sunset and we'd get high and listen to them play music. But with Marina's murder the vibe got too weird. Everyone starting locking their doors and keeping to themselves, giving each other looks and not trusting anyone. No one knew that months later, others would be murdered just like Marina. Overnight, it was like this intense, negative energy had crept in. I was sleeping on a screened-in porch with a flimsy door that wouldn't lock, so I began sleeping with a kitchen knife under my pillow for months, hoping I'd never really have to use it. And just when we were all getting over the shock of Marina's death and settling back into some kind of normalcy, Sharon Tate gets murdered along with others in similar fashion, a hundred stab wounds between them. Then just a few week ago I'm in a coffee shop, watching the news, and I see they caught this guy, Manson, who killed Sharon Tate and her friends. Coincidentally it was the same creepy guy I met through Marina's friend once or twice. He always seemed to be at parties, singing and playing his guitar. Before the murders, the Canyon was like a twenty-four-hour-seven-day-a-week party scene. Lots of chicks, lots of drugs."

"Sounds like the Castle!" I said.

"Not even close."

"I saw that stuff about Manson on the news. What was he like? Did you talk to him a lot?"

"No. The cat made me very uncomfortable. To this day, I'm still having nightmares! He had these wild eyes that seemed to look right through you! And he made up these weird songs he would sing. The chicks were like hypnotized whenever he sang. Before I knew he was an insane killer, I kept thinking to myself the whole time that I wished I had whatever charms the guy had that obviously made him so attractive.

"Do you think he killed Marina?"

"I don't know, and I probably never will. This is really bringing me down. Mind if we talk about something else? So what's been happening with you?"

"I went to Wildwood with Jane last New Year's. Probably the last time I did anything social, unless you want to count playing cards and watching TV with Mrs. Kelly."

Carl smiled, raising his eyebrows. I could see he was wondering if I'd solved my virginity problem.

"Yeah. A hotel room with one double bed." I decided to wait a few seconds more and make him think something might have actually happened with Jane before finishing my sentence. After a short pause I said, "I know what you're thinking, and no, not even a New Year's kiss."

I swear that he looked extremely relieved. "So nothing's happened yet, even with all those nights you spend over at Mrs. Kelly's?" he added jokingly.

I shook my head. "Nothing's going on there either." Then the gypsy woman came to mind with her gold tooth, which I secretly hoped wouldn't be the case every time I thought about women or sex for the rest of my life. I told Carl about her, and how, for some reason I'd never be able to comprehend, she knew I was seeing John, and if I wanted to stop seeing him, I had to burn whatever it was that I took from him, which was nothing I could think of, as far as I knew.

"Gypsy? Heavy stuff. So that shit's still going on?" Carl asked, as he pushed in front of me the peanuts and pretzels sitting on the bar. "You should eat something. You're so pale, man. And you have these dark circles under your eyes. Have you bothered to look at yourself in the mirror lately?"

Even though I had no desire for food, I took some pretzels just to shut him up. "I still see him. I thought that was John singing in my ear when you sneaked up behind me earlier."

"Ha ha! Sorry about that—hey, do you think you guys could still use my help at the marina?"

"I was hoping you'd ask. There's always something we need done, even if the winter isn't as busy. Your boat is still there, too. Do you have somewhere to stay?"

"I saved some bread while I was working at that head shop I told you about. I want to get an apartment soon, but as far as having somewhere to stay right now, I don't. Until I do, I was wondering if I could crash in the boathouse?"

"You should stay at the main house with us. The boathouse is way too cold this time of year."

"I'm used to cold after spending those winters in the Castle. Hey, maybe we should get going? I think Lenny wants to close. I didn't realize we'd been here that long, but it's almost 3 a.m. already!" Carl said, leaving money for our drinks on the bar and telling Lenny we'd see him soon.

Before we went down to the marina, we stopped at the main house where everyone was still asleep, so I could get some soap, towels, blankets and pillows, and a small space heater. I knew that the heater would never be able to heat the tremendous interior of the house barge, but at least the space around where Carl slept would be warm. And unlike the Castle, he'd have electricity for light, too, plus a toilet and shower—even if it was only cold water.

As we headed down the dock, I pointed out to Carl the eaves of the boathouse that were outlined in rows of long, thick icicles like giant crystal weapons ready to strike at random.

"I forgot about those things. You never see them in L.A. Hey, whatever happened to my cat?"

"Ike has him. He brings him to the marina every day. The cat really loves being here. You'll see him later."

"What about Fritz? I bet he loves the cat being here?" Carl laughed.

"They tolerate each other. They actually share a common interest—chasing seagulls—except I think the cat would like to catch one and eat the poor thing rather than have it fly away!"

I began looking through lockers for boat cushions so that Carl could have some kind of makeshift mattress when to my surprise, there in the back of one of the lockers was my brother's little plastic statue of St. Christopher, protector against storms and sudden death. So the statue was here the whole time? Would Will's life have been spared if it was with him that day? He had actually believed the saint saved us all from drowning the day we hit that sunken barge. Maybe he was right, and that was the reason we were saved; maybe there really was something to Catholic charms. The thought occurred to me then that there probably wasn't much difference between Will's little plastic saint and the gypsy's bag of shells. I put the statue in my pocket without mentioning it to Carl.

I got him set up, and then we smoked some of his weed and talked all night until we noticed that the sun was coming up.

"Well, I'm glad you're back," I said. "I better let you get some sleep, though, before Ike gets here." I knew I wouldn't be able to sleep myself, and I had about three more hours until my parents would be awake and Ike would arrive. I walked down to the end of the dock. For the first time since John's death, I stepped down the ladder, its steps still covered in snow, and climbed into my little aluminum rowboat, brushing the snow off one of the seats.

Though the winter was a dangerous this time of year for boating, I rowed out on the river anyway, and I sat for what seemed like hours as I gazed back at the shore while I watched the moon trade places with the bitter cold white sun. Taking the statue from my pocket and then throwing it overboard, I was able to release not only the past but the pent-up anger I'd felt all those years toward the Catholic Church and its insignificant amulets. I watched the saint's image fade as it sank into the filthy blackness of the Hudson. Then I rowed back and stepped out of the boat onto the dock, deliberately leaving it untied...for a second time.

As I climbed the ladder up to the dock, something made me look back at the boat again. Out of the corner of my eye I noticed some kind of movement. The door to the secret compartment Will and I had built was banging open and shut with each passing wave from the incoming tide. I looked in and from the place where I stood on the dock, I could see a plastic bag filled with a lot of cash, which must have been John's half of the bet money.

So this was what I'd had all along that belonged to John. This was what the fortuneteller had been trying to tell me. I guessed then that that was the reason all along that he kept appearing to only me; he'd been trying to tell me to look for the money hidden in my boat and give it to his mom. Maybe that was his way of apologizing to her for leaving her alone, since he hadn't intended for things to work out the way they did. I quickly reached down, pulling on the side of the boat to bring it closer to the dock and climbed back in to retrieve the money. Shivering, I grabbed the bundle of bills, stuffed it in my pocket, and climbed out, pushing the boat as hard as I could with my foot from the dock as I watched it slowly drift away.

Not wanting her to ever know that my boat had anything to do with accident, I decided that I'd walk to Mrs. Kelly's and casually sneak the bundle of cash in with me, placing it in the room where I'd been painting, John's room. I left it up to Mrs. Kelly to find the money on her own, and I was sure she would, in time. Whether or not that would mean finally ridding John from my life, I was willing to take my chances. But as the weeks passed and turned into months, I came to realize that I was finally free.

About the Author

A member of the Bergen County Historical Society, the Gypsy Lore Society and a former graphic artist for Prentice Hall, Lasher Lane has had several short stories published. She lives in Los Angeles with her family but resided for many years in the town she has featured in her debut novel, using the lane she grew up on as her pen name.